Deborah doesn

the perfect bala

— DIANN MILLS, CHRISTY AWARD WINNER

Mrs. Sprinkle's latest *"Whodunit"* has done it again with *The Case of the Stolen Memories!* The author weaves a suspenseful story that immediately draws readers into the mystery and danger that escalates with every twist. This book will keep readers turning pages. Recommended for those who enjoy mystery and suspense novels!

— SANDRA MERVILLE HART, AWARD-
WINNING AUTHOR OF SPIES OF THE CIVIL
WAR SERIES AND SECOND CHANCES SERIES

Deborah Sprinkle does not disappoint—another Sam and Mac adventure that captures the mind with a clever mystery and the heart with authentic relationships.

— LINDA DINDZANS, AUTHOR OF *A
CERTAIN MAN*

THE CASE OF THE
STOLEN
MEMORIES

a mac & sam mystery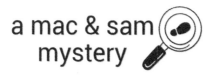

A NOVEL BY
DEBORAH SPRINKLE

Scrivenings
PRESS
Quench your thirst for story.
www.ScriveningsPress.com

To Elizabeth, our beautiful daughter

CHAPTER 1

A voice inside whispered for her to turn around and go back home. Instead, she pulled into a space in the lower parking lot at James W. Rennick Riverfront Park. The world outside was painted in shades of gray, from the slate-colored river gliding past on its way to join the Mississippi above St. Louis to the ashen clouds hanging low on the horizon.

The leafless tree limbs stirred, and Mac shivered. Why did she make New Year's resolutions that required her to get up at the crack of dawn? This year, she resolved to walk two miles three times a week before work. So far, she'd made it a week. If she gave up now ... She got out before she could change her mind.

Mac shrugged into her coat and gloves and headed for the path along the river. As the rhythm of her stride took over, her mind returned to the problem she and her sisters had been wrestling with since November.

Should they claim the inheritance left to them by Rosa Lombardi? It still amazed her how her family's unfortunate history ended up linked to her case of mistaken identity. She'd felt a connection to Rosa beyond their remarkable resemblance, and now she knew why.

The rumble of cars and trucks snapped her back to the present, and the Highway Forty-Seven bridge appeared a quarter mile away. She entered the shadow of the bridge. The familiar noise of the occasional car and the flex of the concrete sounded above her, but today, there was something else—something that made her uneasy. The unease from earlier flooded back, and she slid her hand into the pocket where she kept her pepper spray.

She'd come far enough for today and doubled her tempo until she was well away from the bridge. Where the trail swerved down toward the river and back to her car, she continued straight, into the trees of Rennick Park.

As she passed the old waterworks building, a figure by the Time Capsule Garden caught sight of her, grabbed what looked like a pillowcase, and ran for the parking lot.

"Hey. What are you doing?" Mac charged after him, but he was too far ahead.

He jumped into a dark SUV and peeled out. She let her heart rate settle down before returning to the place where she'd seen him. What was he doing?

The marble top of the Washington, Missouri, Sesquicentennial Time Capsule had been pried off, and the time capsule was empty.

"Peachy. Just peachy." Mac yanked her gloves off and dug her phone out of her sweatpants pocket.

"Nine-one-one. What is your emergency?"

"I'd like to report a robbery."

DETECTIVE JAKE SANDERS wasn't going to respond to the 911 call. In fact, he'd assigned it to Detective Victor Young. But when he heard Mackenzie was the one who called it in, he changed his mind. There were two things he knew about his girlfriend. She couldn't pass up a case, and if she was involved, the case was bound to get messy. He intended to be there to make sure the investigation stayed as orderly as possible.

When he pulled into the park, everything seemed under control for once. Detective Young and Mackenzie were talking to one side, an officer was stringing yellow crime scene tape around the area, and another officer was walking the parking lot, head down, searching for anything useful.

He strolled over to his detective and his girlfriend. "About done?"

"I think I've got everything."

Vic thumbed through his notes and gave Mac a grim smile. "Thanks, Mac. I know you wish you'd been able to catch him in the act, but I'm glad you didn't. The guy had a crowbar. You could have been seriously hurt."

"I guess." She furrowed her brow in the direction of the empty time capsule.

Jake groaned inwardly. Mac would not let this go. "It's cold out here. Let's sit in my car."

She nodded and followed him to his police-issued SUV. Inside, she pulled her gloves off and grabbed a tissue from the box he kept in the console. "The cold makes my nose run. Sorry."

"That's why they're here." A strand of her wavy brown hair kept falling across her face. He leaned over and smoothed it behind her ear.

"You're staring, Jake."

"Can't help it." He grinned as a blush highlighted her cheek bones.

"You just like to get me fluster—"

"Ten fifty-four at the Highway Forty-Seven bridge." Jake's police radio squawked. "All units respond to the lot off Missouri Avenue in back of the Riverview Guesthouse."

"I need to go." Jake buckled his seatbelt.

"I'm coming with you."

"No. Ten fifty-four means a possible dead body."

"I know what it means." She snapped her belt in place. "I want to see if it's related to the robbery."

"Why would you think that?"

"I just have a feeling."

Another one of her feelings. Jake threw the car into gear. Was it always going to be like this? One minute he wanted to kiss her, and the next he wanted to— He shook his head. Nope. Not going there.

Besides, to be honest, many of her feelings turned out to be right. He'd wait to see if this one panned out before starting another argument. Lights and siren on, Jake turned left onto Third Street and prayed he wouldn't meet any teenagers in trucks who thought they could beat him across the intersection.

Across Highway Forty-Seven at the light, a left onto Madison, and another onto Missouri Avenue, and he was there. Several police cars sat in the lot, along with a few other vehicles.

As they pulled to a stop, Mac pointed out the window. "There it is. The SUV I saw this morning." She unfastened her seatbelt and leaped out.

"Are you sure?" Jake raced after her. "Don't touch anything."

She threw him *the Look* before pausing several feet from the vehicle. "I noticed the cracked taillight. See."

Jake greeted the other officers. "What have we got? Man or woman?"

"A man with his head caved in."

Mac drew a sharp breath beside him.

"Who found him?"

"A guy on a bike. He thought it was a drunk sleeping it off until he saw all the blood."

"Where's the guy now?"

"We got his information and let him go. He got sick once and looked pretty shaky."

"Okay." Jake stared in the direction the officer had come from. His questions for the man would have to wait.

"The body's down by the bike path," one patrol officer said. "It's tough to get to. You have to cross the railroad tracks and push through lots of brush. I've got guys cutting a path."

"Can we drive on the bike path?"

"Not wide enough. Especially through the trees."

How did the killer get there? Jake pushed a hand through his hair.

"Have someone search the parking lot for signs of a car leaving in a hurry. Skid marks or something."

The officer cocked an eyebrow at him. "After we've all pulled in here? Do you really think we could tell?"

Jake shrugged. "Worth a shot. The killer had to come from somewhere. Have you taken any photos for the medical examiner?"

"Yeah." The officer handed his phone to Jake.

Mac moved his arm out of the way. "I'm pretty sure he's the guy I saw at the park this morning."

"I thought you didn't get a good look at him." He didn't like guesses.

"I'm good at impressions. I'll know for sure once I see him in person."

"You mean his body." Jake gave her a smug look.

"You know what I meant." Her expression hardened.

"Now tell me about this feeling you had." He pinned her with his gaze. "How did you know the dead guy would be associated with the robbery?"

"It's hard to explain." Her gaze unfocused as she faced the river.

CHAPTER 2

Mac recalled her sense of alarm on her walk earlier in the day. How could she put her sense of unease into words he would understand? In her mind's eye, she imagined the killer lurking in the shadows under the bridge, waiting for the thief to arrive.

A chill skittered down her spine. She'd almost run into a murderer—a much more serious prospect than catching the thief in the act.

"I've been walking along the river in the mornings." Mac faced Jake. "I usually go as far as the bridge and turn around. Sometimes, I go farther. It depends on how I feel."

"And this morning?" Jake asked.

"When I got to the bridge, I felt nervous. Like something bad was about to happen. It spooked me. I turned around and headed back." She sounded irrational to her own ears. How could she expect Jake to take her seriously?

"Good thing you did." He placed a hand on her arm. "Thank God for your intuition."

"You think the killer was hiding under the bridge?"

He nodded. "You could have been ..." He swallowed and stepped closer.

Warmth filled Mac's heart.

"If anything happened to you ..."

A different kind of heat climbed up her throat to her cheeks.

"Ahem," an officer said.

"What is it?" Jake stepped away.

"They're ready to bring the body up, sir."

Four men struggled to roll a gurney up the hill and over the broken pavement. When they drew even with Mac and Jake, they stopped and unzipped the body bag.

"Could you let me see a little more of his clothes?" Mac asked.

One medic opened the bag another six inches.

"Yes. It's him."

Jake motioned for them to cover the body and move on.

"Are you sure?" Jake asked. "Lots of people have similar black jackets."

"I know, but his had a blotch of red, like paint, on the upper left-hand side. My eye was drawn to it. Same as the dead man."

"Good enough for me." Jake rubbed his nose. "It's cold out here. I'll take you back to your car. We need to get this scene processed."

They retraced their route back to the park and Mac's sedan. As they passed the upper lot, she caught a glimpse of the crime scene tape. The morning ran through her mind like a video on a never-ending loop.

"Don't forget the pillowcase." Mac unclicked her belt.

"Pillowcase?"

"The sack he had. With the contents from the time capsule," Mac said. "It looked like a light yellow or tan pillowcase."

"Got it."

"It's the reason he was murdered. I'm sure of it."

"I love how your brain works. See you at the station in an hour," he said.

"Why?"

"For your formal statement, Miss Love."

"Oh yeah." Once again, she found herself in the middle of a case she hadn't expected. "I'll be there."

Mackenzie turned her car on and waited for the heater to overcome the January chill. Should she go home and take a long hot shower, or go to the office and discuss the morning's drama with her partners, Sam and Miss P?

Hot air poured from the vents, and she closed her eyes. Or she could tilt her seat back and take a nap. No, not an option. She put her car in gear and drove the short distance to her office.

Miss Prudence Freebody opened the door before Mac reached it. "Mackenzie, my dear, I'm so glad you're here. We were both so worried. Were you walking in the park this morning?"

She should have called them. Sam and Miss P would have heard about the theft and the body on the police scanner.

"Sorry. I didn't think to call you guys." She shrugged out of her coat and hung it on a hook. "If I'd been a faster walker, I would have caught the guy robbing the time capsule."

"You're kidding." Samantha Majors ran over and grabbed her arm. "I'm glad you're slow."

"Yeah, but if I'd caught him, I may have saved his life because he's the one found dead under the bridge." The full import of her words hit her for the first time, and she plopped into the closest chair. A little sooner, and the thief would be in jail, but alive.

"Maybe," Miss P said. "Or you may have been injured, and he would still be dead. Which is the more likely scenario."

Mac snapped her eyes up to her former chemistry teacher.

"You are a very capable young woman, but sometimes you overestimate your abilities." The older woman's face softened. "I worry about you."

"I don't mean to upset you." Mac shrugged. "I guess I do jump in without thinking—believing I can handle the situation. I'll try to pick my battles more realistically in the future." She picked up her purse and moved to the conference table. "Do we have any coffee?"

"I'll make a fresh pot." Miss P hustled away.

"Sam, grab your computer. I've got some photos I'd like you to download. I managed to get a quick picture of the van as he drove away, and while waiting in the park for the police, I took some shots of the time capsule and surroundings."

"I'm not surprised." The petite blonde woman keyed in a command, and her screen came up. "Ready for airdrop when you are."

The two friends and partners focused on the screen as picture after picture popped up.

"You'll need to rotate a few of these." Mac waved a hand at the computer.

"I was wondering what they were." Sam chuckled.

"Good thinking, Mackenzie." Miss P sat mugs of steaming coffee in front of the two women. "Is that the thief's van?"

"Yes. Can you make it larger?" Mac moved her cup to one side and leaned closer to the screen. "I memorized the first three characters, but not the last three. Jake pulled me away before I got close enough, and if I'd tried to take a picture of it ..."

Sam held her hand up. "We understand." She tapped a few keys and enlarged the photo.

"It's a Missouri plate, right?"

Her partner nodded.

"I can make out TXS. What do you think the rest is?"

"Looks like BRQ?"

"I believe it's BBQ," Miss P said.

"You're right. It's a vanity plate." Mac grinned at her. "Texas Bar B Que. That should make it easier to find the owner."

"I'll start there," Sam said. "After we've looked through the rest of your pictures."

She paused on the photo of the pink marble slab pried from atop the time capsule. A jagged crack ruptured the stone into two pieces. The words TIME CAPSULE To Be Opened 2039 AD were inscribed at the top of one piece with half the sesquicentennial seal. The other half of the seal and SESQ GARDEN were inlaid into the other part of the slab.

Miss P gave a small cry. "Such senseless destruction."

"I know." Sam shook her head. "I mean, what could be in a time capsule worth stealing?"

Mac leaned back and stared at her friends. "The real question is what could be in there worth killing for?"

CHAPTER 3

"I need to go to the station to give Jake my statement." Mac rose. "You two finish going through the photos and see if anything grabs you. I should be back in an hour."

"Tell my brother hello for me." Sam waved a hand at her. "We'll have this all figured out by the time you get back."

"Uh-huh." Mac pulled on her coat and realized she still had on her sweats from her walk this morning, no makeup, and she hadn't washed her hair. "Sam, do me a favor. Call Jake and tell him I'll need another half hour. I'm going home to clean up."

"Why don't you call him?"

"Because he'll argue with me. If you call, what can he say?" Mac grinned and shut the door.

Her phone rang halfway to her house. Jake. She ignored it. Once home, she jumped into the shower, changed, and was back on the road in twenty minutes. A record for her. She texted Jake that she was on her way.

He met her at the glass doors to the Public Safety Building where the police department had its offices, along with the communications center, holding cells, and areas for training.

"I'm sorry, but I couldn't stand being grubby any longer." Mac put a hand up to silence him. "The important thing is I'm here now, and I feel so much better."

"After you." Jake sighed and opened the door.

At the top of the stairs, Mac stopped. A man stood talking to an officer down the hall. "What's Brandon Fischer doing here?"

"He's using our files to help with his search for Rosa Lombardi's heirs."

Mac's mouth went dry. "Is he having any luck?"

"Nothing so far." Jake led the way into his office. "I thought we might grab some lunch after I take your statement. If you have time."

No luck so far. But what could he possibly find here? She massaged her forehead.

"Mackenzie? What's wrong?"

The concern in Jake's voice broke through and brought her back to the here and now.

"I'm sorry. I zoned out for a minute." She smiled at him. "What were you saying?"

"I asked if you'd want to have lunch after we talk, but if you're not feeling well, we can do it another day."

"No." She waved a dismissive hand at him. "I'm fine. I'd love to have lunch with you."

"Okay." Jake pulled his computer over. "Let's get started. When did you arrive at the park?"

"Around six-thirty."

"Did you notice any other cars?"

"I parked in the lower lot. There weren't any where I was, but I didn't pay any attention to the upper lot."

"You took the river trail. Right?" Jake asked.

She nodded.

Jake continued to question her, and she answered, leaving

out the fact she took photos of the scene. Or that she intended to investigate on her own.

"I think that's all we need for now." He closed his laptop. "Where would you like to go for lunch?"

"The Tilted Skillet. I love their burger and fries." Mac licked her lips.

"Let's go."

They arrived at a busy time, but a couple walked away from a window table, and they pounced on it. The busboy hurried over.

"Hi, Detective, Mac." He piled dishes onto a tray. "You guys lucked out. I'll tell your waiter to get over here."

"No rush." Jake reached for Mac's hand across the small table. "I know you're going to look into the robbery and murder on your own."

He knew her so well. Was that good or bad?

"I'd rather we work together. You tell me if you find anything, and I'll do the same."

"Okay." She withdrew her hand. "Whose van was it?"

"Good question. The plates were stolen. They came back to a Cadillac." Jake rubbed the bridge of his nose. "Probably the van was stolen as well."

Her spirits fell. Putting a name to the dead man wasn't going to be so easy.

"Have you identified the body yet?" she asked.

"No." Jake shook his head. "Vic's checking fingerprints, but if he's not in the system, we'll have to rely on missing persons and maybe dental records."

"Sorry to keep you waiting." A waitress with a mass of blonde curls pulled back in a ponytail bustled over. "What can I get for you?" She looked up from her order book. "Mac? Is that you?"

"Zoe?" Mac jumped up and hugged the woman. "This is Detective Jake Sanders."

"I know Jake." The blonde woman winked at him. "I've waited on him a time or two."

Mac cast a curious glance at Jake, who hadn't seemed to notice. Hmm. She returned her attention to Zoe. "I thought you'd got married and moved away."

"I did, but the jerk left me, and now I'm back. Waitressing." The woman indicated her T-shirt with the Tilted Skillet logo stretched over an ample chest.

"I'm sorry to hear that, but it's good to see you." Mac picked up her menu. "I'll have a burger, medium well, and sidewinder fries with salt and pepper. Easy on the pepper. And an iced tea."

"Got it." The waitress turned to Jake with a broad smile. "Your usual, Detective?"

"I'll have what Mac's having."

The smile faded from Zoe's face, and she closed her order book. "I'll get that right out."

Mac watched her high school friend walk away. "I think you have an admirer, Jake."

"Who?" He glanced around.

"Zoe, you goofball." Men could be so dense.

"She's a nice girl, but she's nice to everybody." He gave a half shrug. "Besides, I'm taken."

Warmth climbed her neck to her cheeks.

"Here you go." Zoe appeared at their table with the ice teas. "What are you doing these days, Mac?"

"Samantha Majors, Jake's sister, and I are private investigators. We have our own business."

"Wow. I've always been interested in that kind of work." She looked at Jake. "In fact, I've applied to the police force."

"Good for you," Jake said.

"I hope I get in." Zoe glanced over her shoulder. "I'm not sure how much longer this job will last. Since Covid, things have been tight, and the landlord raised the rent on the building."

Mac looked around the restaurant. Almost every table was full, but it probably wasn't always like this. So many businesses closed during the pandemic, and afterwards, many that thought they could make it ended up in receivership. Could Zoe be right about the Tilted Skillet? Or was she just spreading gossip?

Mac spied another customer staring their way. "I think they need you over there." She nodded in the direction of the other table.

Zoe raised a finger at the man to indicate she'd be there in a minute. "We'll have to get together some time when I'm not working." She grinned at Mac.

"That would be great." Mac smiled back but felt a stone in the pit of her stomach. Was she ready to renew the relationship? They hadn't been close before, and now that she was single again, it seemed like Zoe might be interested in Jake. That would never do.

But on the other hand, the woman had moved back after a nasty divorce and could use a friend. "I'll give you my number."

Zoe's grin became a smile that lit up her face. "I'll be back soon with your food."

Mac stared out the window. *Lord, help me. I don't have the strength to take on another woman's personal problems right now.*

"Hey." Jake touched her hand. "What's up?"

"It's just ..." She sighed. "I'm feeling pretty overwhelmed with my own stuff right now."

"It's up to you how much time you spend with her," Jake said. "Or how close you get."

"But I don't want to be mean."

"I'm not saying be mean. I'm saying set healthy boundaries."

Mac met Jake's steady gaze. "How did you get so wise?"

Their food arrived in a savory cloud of aromas that made her mouth water, and she forgot about her woes and work for a brief time. Another thing she liked about Jake. When the food came, all talk stopped, and they enjoyed their meal.

As he swallowed his last bite, Jake snatched his cellphone from his pocket. "Sanders." He flashed a look at Mac. "Be there in twenty minutes."

CHAPTER 4

"What was that about?" Mac asked.

"I need to get back to the murder scene." Jake motioned to Zoe, who came over with their bill—which she handed to Jake.

"Oh." Mac looked from her friend to Jake. "We usually go dutch."

"Sorry." Zoe reached for the paper. "I thought you guys were ..."

"We are." Jake handed Zoe some cash. "I'll pay this time." He looked at Mac. "You can pay for our next meal. Ready?"

Mac and Jake climbed into his SUV, and as he pulled away from the curb, she pressed the button on her phone to call Samantha.

"Hi, Mac. How was lunch?"

"Good." Mac raised an eyebrow. How did Sam know she'd gone to lunch with Jake? "I'm on my way back to the murder scene with Jake."

He pricked her with a frosty look.

She ignored him. "How did you know I'd had lunch with Jake?"

"I called the station looking for you." A chuckle came over the phone. "What? Do you think I'm a mind reader too? Jake says that all the time."

Sometimes it seemed that way, but she'd never tell Sam. "Nay." She scoffed for Sam's benefit. "I knew it had to be something like that. See you later."

"What makes you think you're coming with me to the crime scene?"

"Because I'm a good investigator, and we work well together." She gave him her most dazzling smile. "Right?"

"And you'll find a way in no matter what I do so I might as well take you."

"That too."

"Mac, what you say is true. You are a good investigator. The best. And we do work well together." He bounced over the curb into the parking lot at the police station. "But you're a witness. You can't come with me to the murder scene."

"Seriously?" She stared at him. "You're not taking me with you?"

"I'm not taking you with me. I shouldn't have taken you this morning."

Irritation curdled her stomach. "Fine." She undid her belt and reached for the door latch.

The touch of his hand on her arm dissolved her frustration, and she sat back with a sigh.

"I get it. I don't like it, but I get it." She cocked her head at him. "Promise you'll call me with details about what you find?"

"Let's go for ice cream at Main Street Creamery later." He brushed a wisp of hair away from her face. "I'll catch you up over a sundae."

"Sounds good."

THIS WAS one of the most inconvenient murder scenes Jake had ever been to. After some thought, he decided to use four-wheelers to travel back and forth from the park to where the body was found.

Detective Victor Young met him in the parking lot. "You okay riding double?"

"Sure. As long as you're driving."

They climbed on one of the bigger machines and took off. Once there, Jake took a moment to survey the scene. The riverfront bikeway trail stretched into the distance in both directions. Noise from the cars on the bridge overhead echoed in the semi-enclosed space, and trash caught in the crushed dead grasses of winter blended with the dirt. A dreary place to die. Not that there was a good place to be murdered.

"What did you bring me here to see?"

"The forensics guys found what they think are the tracks of the killer's bicycle." Vic walked along the edge of the trail. About six feet east of the crime scene, he stooped down and pointed to a yellow marker.

"What makes them so certain this track is the killer's compared to all the others?"

"They say it's the most recent."

"Have you followed it?"

"Yes. He stopped here for a moment and walked across the trail toward the river." Vic indicated a partial shoe print. "Maybe to take a ... you know."

"Did they find any biological fluid?"

"No."

"Are they done searching the area?"

"As far as I know."

Jake stepped slowly through the dry, brittle vegetation and piles of damp leaves, his eyes raking the ground. The bare limbs of the trees stirred above him. Why would the killer have taken precious time to stop at this spot? What was so urgent? To change clothes? Did he take a leak, or pretend to in order to let someone pass? He raised his gaze.

A spot of color on the edge of the river caught his eye. "Over here." He pushed forward a few feet.

"What is it?" Vic arrived at his side.

"It looks like a piece of cloth. Get forensics back here."

Detective Young raised his phone to his ear. "We need you guys at the riverside murder scene pronto."

Jake took a few cautious steps closer.

"Hang on," Vic said. "The team should be here soon."

"What color would you say that is?"

"I don't know. Hard to tell from here." Vic blew into his hands. "Probably some old shirt a fisherman lost. I wish those guys would hurry up."

"Yeah." But the cold didn't register with Jake right now, and his instincts told him this wasn't a rag.

"Detectives?" Two men in white coveralls approached. "What have you got for us?"

"Over there. In the weeds by the river." Jake pointed in the direction of the piece of cloth.

Forensics moved in on the spot in stages, starting from where Jake was standing and checking the ground for evidence. After ten to fifteen minutes, one man lifted the fabric and looked back at Jake and Vic. "It's a pillowcase."

"Okay. Good." Jake rolled his shoulders to relieve his tension. "Bring it here."

"There's something inside." One man put in a gloved hand

and withdrew a rock. "This might be your murder weapon." He bagged the rock and the pillowcase separately before joining Jake and Vic.

"I don't think it's the murder weapon," Vic said.

"Looks like blood on the rock." Jake peered through the plastic evidence bag.

"The coroner's report just came through. The guy died of stab wounds to the chest and back."

"So, who's blood is on the rock?" One of the forensics men asked.

"Good question." Jake handed the bag back. "Did you find any evidence other than the pillowcase?"

"Only these." The man handed him three baggies. "This one looks like the corner off a kid's drawing, and this might be part of a photograph. The other's a crushed cigarette box."

Adrenaline shot through Jake once more. A picture of what happened here was forming in his mind.

"Were they close to where you found the pillowcase?"

"No. Closer to where you were standing."

He nodded.

"What are you thinking?" Vic asked.

"The killer stopped here to transfer the stuff from the pillowcase into a backpack or something like that." Jake walked to where he'd stood before, and Vic followed. "He put the rock in the pillowcase and heaved it toward the river. When he heard the splash, he assumed he'd gotten it all the way, but the pillowcase only made it into the shallows. Waves from the barges pushed it farther up on shore."

"And he got on his bike and rode off." Vic turned to look once more at the bicycle path. "We need to question people about seeing anyone with a backpack riding a bicycle this morning."

"Or saddlebags?" Jake asked. "Do they still make those things?"

"Don't know, but I'll find out," Vic said. "Maybe the items from the time capsule could be made to fit into a small space. Like a fanny pack."

"Good point. We need to find out what was in the capsule." Jake scratched his nose. "And why someone would want to steal it."

CHAPTER 5

Mackenzie drove through the bleak January day, the heavy clouds pressing on her spirit. So many things weighed on her heart. As much as it stung for Jake to refuse to take her to the murder scene, he had done her a favor. She had no business trying to catch a thief and a murderer on her own time. Not to mention bringing Sam and Miss P in on it too. Money was tight again, and they needed a new case—one that paid.

If she and her sisters claimed Rosa Lombardi's inheritance, the company's money woes would be over. But it would mean exposing her family skeletons, and she wasn't sure she was ready to do that.

Mac pulled into the driveway next to the office, shut off the car, and laid her forehead on the steering wheel. *Lord, I need your guidance.*

As Mac entered the building, Sam brandished the office phone. "We've got a possible client on the phone."

Mac whispered a quiet thanks and hung up her coat. "Who is it?"

"Tim Koenig from the Meerschaum pipe museum?" Sam cocked her shoulder. "He says he's calling in the favor."

Tim Koenig? An image of a short, stocky man with glasses standing behind the counter of the museum filled her mind.

"I do owe him a favor." Mac joined Sam at the conference table. "He helped us with the Eleanor Davis case, and I recognized him from Sunday school, but I couldn't remember his name. Put him on speaker."

"Mr. Koenig, Ms. Love is here along with our assistant, Ms. Freebody. Go ahead."

"Ms. Love, you remember saying if I ever needed you to call?"

"Yes." Mac folded her arms on the table and stared at the phone. "What's the problem, Tim?"

"I'd rather talk in person. Are you free, or can I make an appointment?"

"We could see you in about ... an hour." Mac traded a glance with Sam, who nodded.

"Great." The relief in his voice resonated through the speaker. "Thank you."

Miss P stood. "I'll make a new pot of coffee and put some of my homemade muffins on a plate."

"Before you go, I wanted to let you know what I learned from Jake at lunch." Mac pulled her writing tablet in front of her. "We can forget about getting an identification through the license plates. They were stolen, and probably the van too. In fact, I've decided it's pointless for us to spend time searching for the thief and his killer."

"Mackenzie, it's not like you to back away from a case." Miss P peered at her over her glasses. "Especially one you have a personal interest in."

"You're not giving up because Jake refused to take you to the crime scene, are you?" Sam asked.

"You know me better than that." Mac threw her a bristly look. "I'm trying to be more responsible and considerate of you guys."

"And we appreciate it, my dear." Miss P patted her on the arm.

"Time to take care of emails." Mac scooped up her phone and huffed off.

When she booted her computer, the photo of her and Ivy, her childhood friend, as kids swinging at the park, appeared as her screensaver. A sigh escaped her lips. Yet another subject that weighed on her heart. After all those years building a friendship, learning part of it was a lie had left Mac questioning her relationships with everyone. What else was she misreading or missing all together?

She tapped a series of commands and changed her screensaver to a picture taken last Thanksgiving. Three heads —brown, gray, and blonde—all in a row, represented three women. Beth, the oldest, stood in the middle, her prematurely gray hair touching her shoulders. Grinning from ear to ear, Kate, the middle child, was on Beth's lefthand side with Mac to Beth's right.

So dissimilar, yet there was something about the three women that revealed their sisterhood. As Mac gazed at the photo, joy and thankfulness pushed out the melancholy and worry that darkened her soul. Somehow she knew it would all work out.

"May I come in?" Sam cracked the door to Mac's office.

She nodded and flashed her partner a smile.

"I'm sorry." Sam stood beside the desk. "I didn't mean to make you angry."

"I know." Mac rose and gave her friend a hug. "I'm kind of touchy today."

"What's going on? Is it my crazy brother again?"

"Yes and no." Mac avoided Sam's compassionate look. She wasn't prepared to share her dilemma about the inheritance with her friend. "At first, I was angry with him for not taking me to the crime scene, but I realized it was for the best. We don't need to be drawn into another case that doesn't have a paycheck promised at the conclusion."

"We've managed before. We could do it again." Sam placed a hand on her arm. "If you want to go after the killer, we will. Besides, somehow we seemed to have made a little money from those cases even when we didn't expect it."

"True." Mac barked a laugh. "I guess we must be doing something right." Her face sobered. "But I'd rather not push it. Let's stick with cases where we know there's a check at the end."

"Speaking of which, Tim Koenig should be here any minute." Sam peered in the mirror by Mac's office door. "Do I look all right?"

"You're fine." Mac leaned in close and ran her fingers over her face. "Move over. I've got some serious repairs to do."

"I'll tell him you'll be a little late."

Mac swatted at her but missed. A chime sounded as the front door opened. The partners glanced at each other.

"I'll get him settled." Sam slipped out of the office.

Mac smoothed some moisturizer on her face and brushed mascara on her lashes. A touch of lipstick and blush, and she squared her shoulders. She was ready to do business. She hoped.

As she came into the main room, a man rose from the sofa. His disheveled brown hair fell over his narrow forehead, and his glasses slid down his slim nose. She flashed back to the day she saw him at the Meerschaum pipe museum. He'd lost weight, and his face looked haggard.

"Mr. Koenig, good to see you again." Mac strode forward, hand outstretched.

He shoved his glasses up his nose and took her hand. "You too. Call me Tim."

"And I'm Mac. You've met Samantha." She gestured toward her partner. "And Miss Freebody?"

He nodded.

"Let's sit at the conference table so we can take notes." She sat in her usual chair at the head with Sam to her left. Miss P pulled a chair out for Tim to Mac's right.

"Would anyone like coffee or iced tea?" Miss P remained standing, hands folded in front of her.

"I'll take a glass of tea." Sam raised a hand.

"Me too." Mac waved a finger as she turned her attention to her notepad.

"Mr. Koenig?"

"Have you got a soda?" He shifted on his chair and adjusted his glasses.

"Diet or regular?"

"Regular."

Mac darted a look in his direction. Anxiety exuded from every pore of the man seated next to her. This wasn't the same man she remembered from the museum, the man who defied orders to help her. She stopped writing.

"Why don't you tell us why you're here." Mac gave him a smile meant to relax and encourage him, but if anything, he seemed more nervous.

"Maybe I made a mistake." He shot them a look filled with uncertainty and fear. "I don't want to waste your time. I should go."

Mac placed a hand on his arm. "I tell you what. You tell us what's been troubling you, and we'll decide together whether it's something you need to worry to about or something we can help you with. Okay? No commitments either way. Just talking."

His brows drew together over the rim of his glasses as he pondered what she'd said. After a long moment, his face cleared, and the tension seemed to bleed away from him. "I'd like that. I haven't had anybody to talk to."

"We're good listeners." Sam graced him with one of her beautiful smiles.

"I don't know where to start."

Miss P handed out iced teas, placed a glass of soda within Tim's reach, and took her seat. "I've always found it's best to start at the beginning."

"I guess that would be when our mom died, and Freddy and me were left on our own. Him being the oldest, he had to take care of me." Tim gulped about a third of his soft drink before continuing. "Somehow he managed to pay the bills. I was young and never asked how. Later, I didn't want to know how."

"You think he was doing something illegal?" Sam stopped taking notes and looked at him.

"I don't think it was exactly illegal, but it probably pushed the boundaries."

"Go on."

"I grew up and started working. Got my own place, and we sold the house." Tim shoved the hair off his face, but it fell back. "Freddy and me didn't see as much of each other. We kept in touch, but ..."

"That happens as we get older." Mac remembered how hard it was when her sisters got married and started their own lives. "You get used to it."

"Yeah." He nodded. "But two years ago, Freddy came over to my house and told me he had a job offer in St. Louis with a construction firm. It sounded great. Like he was finally doing something with his life."

"Was?" Something in his tone pinched Mac in her gut.

"He left, and I didn't hear from him for a long time. I tried to get in touch, but he never returned my calls or texts, and I didn't have an email for him. Until ..."

"Go on."

"A week ago, he called to say he was coming home." Tim turned haunted eyes toward her. "And that's the last I've heard or seen of him."

"What have you done to try to find him so far?" Mac prayed the urgency she felt hadn't come through in her words.

"I tried calling until his phone went ... lost its charge." Tim took off his glasses and rubbed his eyes. "I called the train depot in Kirkwood to see if he bought a ticket. It took some fancy talking, but I finally got them to tell me he had."

"Were you able to confirm he arrived in Washington?"

"No. I couldn't convince anyone to give me that information."

"We can find out. If you want us to." Mac made a note.

"You think I'm not being stupid?" Tim said, his voice made husky with unshed tears. "What if Freddy is involved in some scheme and finds out I hired private investigators?"

"You just tell him he should be glad he has a brother who loves him enough to care so much." This time she did let her irritation show. But her instincts whispered that Freddy's days of skirting the law were probably past.

"Do you have a picture of your brother?"

Tim rummaged in his jacket pocket and withdrew a crumpled photograph. He laid it on the table and smoothed it with care. "This is him. My brother, Freddy."

Mac took the photo and pressed her lips together to stop the cry that rose in her throat.

CHAPTER 6

M ac cut her eyes to Tim, who had his head down, and passed the photo to Sam. She heard a small intact of breath, covered by a soft cough. What should they do?

"I think we may be able to help you, Tim." Sam stood. "Why don't you go home and let us make some inquiries? We'll call you in a couple of days with a report."

Thank God Sam kept her head and took the lead. Mac pushed to her feet, a lump the size of a lemon seemed lodged in her throat, making it impossible for her to speak.

"Are you sure?" He rose and scanned their faces.

"I'm sure. If we don't find anything, we won't charge you." Sam took his arm and walked him to the door. "Does that seem fair?"

"Yes. Very fair." He pumped Sam's hand. "God bless you."

Mac watched through the front window as he drove away, her stomach churning. "I couldn't tell him. Not before we check to make sure."

"No." Sam put an arm around her friend. "Let's go. The sooner we know, the better."

"May I see the photograph?" Miss P stood behind them.

Sam held it out to her.

"Oh dear." The older woman placed a hand on her heart. "Yes, you must be sure before saying anything to this poor young man."

Miss P handed the photo to Mac, who stared at the image. The face of the dead thief smiled back at her.

"Time to rock and roll, girlfriend." Sam gave Mac's arm a gentle tug.

"Ladies, for what it's worth, I remember these boys from school." Miss P paused while gathering the empty glasses. "Freddy was a difficult young man. One who constantly pushed the boundaries." She took off her glasses and rubbed the bridge of her nose. "There was something else about the boys, but I can't quite bring it to mind. I'll have to think about it while you're away."

For the second time that day, Mac steered her car toward the police department on the corner of Third and Jefferson. "I don't know if I want Freddy to be the thief or not. On the one hand, Tim would know what happened to his brother, but on the other, he'd find out his brother was a thief working for someone else who killed him."

"If he's not the thief, Tim is left wondering what happened to his brother, and that's not good either."

Mac shut the car off and turned to Sam. "I hate cases like these."

"So do I, my friend."

"Let's get this over with." Mac exited her car and trudged up the sidewalk, head down against the biting wind.

"Hey, wait for me." Sam caught up with her.

They shed their gloves in the foyer and their coats at the top of the stairs. That was the problem with winter. It was too cold outside and too hot inside. Perspiration formed along her neck under her hair.

"What can I do for you, ladies?" the receptionist said.

"Is my brother around?" Samantha swiped a hand across her forehead.

"He just got back. I'll let him know you're here."

"Thanks."

Mac and Sam stepped away from the desk and out of earshot of the woman sitting there.

"I see you're glistening too." Mac let out a low chuckle. "Why do they keep this place so warm?"

"I have no idea."

"Detective Sanders said to go on back," the receptionist said.

Once in Jake's office, Mac laid the photograph of Freddy Koenig on an open file in front of him.

"Where'd you get this?" Jake snatched the picture off his desk and gave them a perplexed look.

"From a potential client." Mac perched on the edge of a chair near his desk. "Tim Koenig. This is his brother, Freddy, and Tim came to us for help because he's missing."

"What do you think, bro?" Sam came around to peer over Jake's shoulder. "Could this be the murder victim?"

Jake stood and walked to the window, photo in hand. "Sure looks like him to me."

"We thought so too." Satisfaction at being able to give the dead man a name warred inside Mac with sorrow at having to tell Tim about his brother.

"We'll need to talk to your client. Get a sample of his brother's DNA if possible or dental records to make a positive ID." Jake placed the picture to one side on his desk. "I'm sorry, Mac."

She waved away his kind words. "I'll text you his address

and phone number." She needed to treat this like any other case. "Anything new on the murder?"

Jake ran a hand through his hair.

"You promised to keep me posted. Remember?"

"I know." He sat and scanned the file in front of him. "We found bicycle tracks we think belong to the killer, leading away from the scene. At one point, he stopped, and it appears he transferred the contents of the pillowcase into another container. Maybe a backpack."

"So, I was right about the pillowcase?" Mac high fived herself internally.

"Yes. We found it by the river's edge." Jake closed the file as if he slammed a door and locked it.

Mac eyed him. "What aren't you telling us?"

"This isn't your case. Good to see you both." He stood. "Mac, we still on for ice cream later?"

"Sure, Jake." She forced her pinched lips into a sweet smile. Another chance to wheedle it out of him later.

Outside, Sam confronted her. "What happened to dropping the theft and murder case? We can't afford to take on cases that don't pay anymore."

"I forgot." Warmth crept up Mac's neck to her face. "I get caught up in the moment, and you know."

"I do. All too well." Sam stormed off.

A tense silence poisoned the air as they drove back to the office. As soon as Mac pulled into the driveway, Sam slammed out of the car. She'd never seen her partner so angry. It hurt her soul.

"Sam?" Now it was Mac knocking on Sam's door, begging forgiveness. What a day. "Please forgive me. You're my best friend. I couldn't do this without you. Let me come in."

A muffled answer sounded through the door, which Mac

took for okay. She opened the door to find Sam, head down on her arms, sobbing her eyes out. "Sammy, what's the matter?"

"I'll be okay." Sam grabbed a handful of tissues. "It's just I'm so thankful you ask me to go in with you on this business, and I love it. But money is tight, and it has me worried."

"I know."

"I'm not sure you do. Not really." Sam opened her computer and logged onto their bank account. "Here's all we have to last us until we get another paying case."

Mac's heart sunk into her stomach. Things were worse than she realized.

"When you came in this morning, declaring we were not getting involved in the time capsule theft and murder, I can't tell you how thrilled I was." Sam raised her arms in the air. "I thought, finally, she gets it." She dropped her arms into her lap. "But with Jake this afternoon, I realized I was wrong."

"No." Mac shook her head emphatically. "I do get it, and I promise you no more cases without a paycheck."

"What do we do about Tim? Do we charge him for time spent?"

Mac sunk into the chair next to Sam. "What do you think?"

The friends shared a dejected look.

"I vote no," Sam said.

"Me too."

"But we've got to spend a little money on marketing. We need clients."

"I agree." Mac pushed to her feet. "Let's get Miss P on that." Her cellphone vibrated in her pocket. An unknown number flashed on her screen. Usually, she'd let it go to voicemail, but for some reason, she felt compelled to answer.

"Mackenzie Love, Private Investigator. How may I help you?"

"Miss Love, this is Hank Young, the Director of Parks and Recreation for Washington. I have a job for you."

CHAPTER 7

J ake did a fist pump as he hung up the phone in his office. They found a witness, and he was on his way into the precinct. Maybe this would be the break he needed. He raised his head at a knock on his door. Detective Victor Young, no doubt.

But it wasn't Vic—unless he was in disguise. A shapely young woman with luxurious blonde curls falling to her shoulders stepped in. She looked familiar, but it took Jake a moment to recognize Zoe from the Tilted Skillet. He jumped to his feet.

"I hope I'm not bothering you." Her wide eyes fixed on his in an innocent look.

But something inside warned him she wasn't as naïve as she appeared. "No. Have a seat. What can I do for you?" He cringed inside. Wrong choice of words, but was there a right choice?

"I wanted to share my good news." She pressed her hands together. "I made it into police academy."

"Great."

"Maybe someday we'll be working together."

"Possibly." He drew the word out and put on a non-committal smile. Mac would love that. Not.

"Well, that's all." She stood and looked at him expectantly.

"Thanks for coming by." He pushed to his feet and walked around his desk.

Before he knew what happened, she grabbed him, pressed herself against him in a hug, and kissed him on the lips. "You have been my inspiration to try for this. I can't thank you enough."

Stunned, Jake stared at her. What just happened?

"See you later." She winked at him and slipped out the door just as Vic entered.

"Who was that?" The detective whistled as he watched Zoe leave. When he caught sight of Jake, he barked a laugh. "You all right?"

"Fine." Jake glared at him and yanked his shirt sleeves down. "Is the witness here yet?"

"Waiting in the interview room. You going to tell me who she is?"

"Zoe something. She came by to tell me she made it into the police academy." Jake headed down the hall with Vic trailing after.

"Uh-huh. I see."

"No, you don't. She's a friend of Mac's." Warmth climbed Jake's neck. He'd have to tell Mac about Zoe's visit, and soon, or she was bound to hear about it from all the loose lips in town.

"I never thought anything else." Vic held the door to the interview room for Jake.

A slim middle-aged man with a receding hairline sat along the wall. He looked up as the door opened.

"This is Mr. Charles Amory."

"Hello, sir. I'm Detective Jake Sanders. You've met Detective Young. We would like to go through your statement with you again. I know it seems tedious, but the mind is funny. The more times we go over things, the more details we seem to remember."

"Where should I begin?" The man rubbed a hand over his sparse hair.

"Why were you out at that time of day?"

"I'm on disability from my job because of a car accident I was involved in. My doc said to walk several times a day. So, I take my dog to the bicycle path. This time of year, there aren't many people out. Especially when it's this cold."

"Did you see anyone else?"

"No. I was alone." He shifted in his chair. "Until the guy on the bike nearly ran me over."

"When was this?"

"About eight-thirty?" He pointed to his wrist. "I didn't wear my watch."

"Okay." Jake glanced at his notes. It fit with the time of death. "What do you remember about the man? You're sure it was a man?"

"I never thought about that." Amory gave them a sharp look. "I guess it could have been a woman, but she would have to be athletic. The person pumped the bike hard and was traveling fast."

"Go on."

"What are you looking for?"

"Was it a mountain bike or a racer? What color was it? What was the rider wearing? Things like that." Jake rubbed the spot on his forehead where a tension headache threatened to form.

Mr. Amory closed his eyes in concentration. "I don't know much about bikes, but it was regular size. The tires were too fat to be a racer, and it was a dark color. That's the best I can do. The rider had on a ski mask, dark jacket, and shiny, tight pants like skiers wear. They had some red in them."

"Did the person on the bike seem tall, short, or average?"

"How do you tell?"

"Were his arms and legs long?"

"Not that I noticed. His legs seemed skinny, but they didn't seem long or short. I couldn't say about his arms because of his coat."

"Good. Anything else?"

"I told your officer the bike had saddlebags on the back. I didn't know they still made those things."

Relief flooded through Jake's body. Not much but something.

"Hang on. I do remember something else." Mr. Amory straightened. "Maybe it was a woman. There was a light-colored ponytail sticking out from under the back of his—or her—ski mask."

"Excellent." Vic's face glowed with enthusiasm. "Blonde?"

"Kind of." Amory shook his head. "But not real light. More what I call dishwater blonde."

"Anything else? Maybe a logo on the back of his jacket?"

"Sorry. Nothing."

"Fine." Jake stood and offered his hand. "If you think of anything else, please call. This officer will escort you out."

Mr. Amory shook hands with Jake and Vic. "I've never been on this side of things before."

"What do you mean?"

"Some years ago, I was a police officer back East. You guys have a tough job."

"Washington, Missouri, is a little quieter than where you worked." Jake barked a laugh. "But it still gets interesting."

After Amory left, Jake looked at Vic. "What's dishwater blonde?"

"Dark blonde or light brown." Vic shrugged. "My mom said my sister's hair was that color. It's kind of an old term."

"What do we know about our perp?"

"He's average height and weight." Vic held up his index finger. "He's strong." He raised a second finger. "He's got long dark blond hair."

"And he could be a she." Jake blew out his cheeks and released them in a sigh. "Not much to go on."

"But more than we had."

Jake nodded. "At least I've got a lead on the victim." He withdrew the picture of Freddy Koenig and handed it to Vic.

"This is him. Who is he?"

Jake related Mac and Sam's afternoon visit to him. "It's too late now, but first thing tomorrow, I want to knock on his door, and I want you to go along." He glanced at the clock. "Now, I have to meet a girl about an ice cream." And try to sweeten their relationship again.

CHAPTER 8

Mac raised her eyebrows at Sam. Her breath snagged in her throat, and it took her a moment to answer.

"Miss Love? Are you there?"

"Yes, Mr. Young. Let me transfer you to our office phone so my associates can be in on the call as well." Mac pressed some buttons, and the office phone rang. Sam picked up and pressed speaker. "Mr. Young?"

"I'm here."

Mac hung up her cellphone and prayed she wouldn't lose the call altogether. The three women huddled around the speaker on the conference table. "We're all here, Mr. Young. My partner, Samantha Majors."

"Hello, Mr. Young."

"And our associate, Miss Prudence Freebody."

"Miss Freebody, my chemistry teacher?"

"The same, Henry Young," Miss P said.

"My son, Victor, recommended your agency, but now I'm certain I'm in good hands." The crinkle of paper sounded over the speaker. "I'll get right to it. I want to hire your firm to find the memorabilia from the time capsule and get it back. Whatever it takes. We'll pay your going rate."

"Sir, the police are already working on the case and are close to identifying the thief. I'm not turning down a job, but why do you want us to do what the authorities are already doing?"

"Because they are more interested in catching the thief and identifying the murdered man and killer than they are in recovering the stolen memories." His voice elevated with every word. "I want you to be our representative, our advocate, our champion in this whole affair."

Mac looked at her partner and associate, who both nodded. How could they turn down a much-needed paying case? It was a blessing. "We'll be glad to take your case, Mr. Young. Would you be available to come by the office tomorrow for a meeting?"

"What time?"

"Nine o'clock in the morning?"

"I'll be there."

"Please bring a list of the items placed in the time capsule so we know what to look for." Sam tapped on her computer.

The line was quiet. "That may be difficult. The woman in charge of memorabilia passed away. I'll see if I can find her original list somewhere in the files."

Mac linked eyes with Sam. Were they once again getting in over their heads? How could they possibly find the stolen memories if they had no idea what they were?

"I understand the importance of the information. I'll do all I can to provide you with a list of the contents of the time capsule. See you tomorrow morning."

As Mac pressed End, she let out a groan. "I hope he finds the list, or this may be the hardest case we've ever taken on."

"Yes." A smile sat lightly on Miss P's face. "But I've taught many people in this town and have many connections. I'm sure I can be of service if a list cannot be produced."

Sam danced around the table and gave the older woman a hug. "We're so blessed to have you."

Mac placed a hand on her arm. "Yes, we are." She caught sight of the time. "I have an ice cream date with your brother in a couple of hours, but first we need to speak with Tim Koenig."

Sam's blue eyes clouded with concern. After a brief conversation, she put her phone down. "He's on his way."

"I'll make a fresh pot of coffee." Miss P stood and crossed to the kitchen doorway.

"You'll need to take the lead on this one." Sam pulled a tissue from the box and wiped her eyes. "I'm not sure I can stand to be here at all. It's too sad."

"Okay." Mac prayed for the guidance and the right words, or else she'd be a blubbering mess as well.

The door opened, and both women rose to greet Tim Koenig. Miss P walked into the room with a mug, bringing the rich scent of Columbian brewed coffee.

"Let's sit on the couches, Tim." Mac indicated the reception area of the large room.

His face became guarded, and he lowered himself carefully onto the edge of a loveseat. Miss P sat the mug within his reach.

"Did you find Freddy?"

"We did." Mac sat across from him and took a quiet breath. "I'm sorry to have to tell you—he's dead."

The grief-stricken man lowered his head. "I was afraid of that, but I hoped he was just off getting in trouble."

"He was kind of doing both. Only this time, his trouble caught up with him."

"What do you mean?" Tim raised his tear-stained face to stare at Mac.

"Freddy was the one who broke into the time capsule, and the one who was killed under the bridge."

"Idiot." Tim grabbed his head with his hands and flopped back on the couch. "I told him to stay away from those guys. I knew he'd end up hurt or ..."

"Tim." Mac moved next to him on the couch. "The police are going to want to talk to you."

"Me?" He straightened. "Why? I didn't have anything to do with this."

"They'll need some things only you can give them. Like DNA samples and a list of his known associates."

"I can't help them with any of that."

"All the same. They'll need a positive ID from you." Mac placed a hand on his arm. "Do you want me to get you an attorney?"

"No." He sighed. "I'll be okay. The only thing I might need help with is when it comes time to bury him."

"We can do that."

He looked at her and Sam and Miss P. "How much do I owe you?"

Tears flooded Sam's eyes, and she rushed from the room.

"You don't owe us anything. We didn't do any work."

"Are you sure?"

"Positive."

He gave her an awkward hug. "Thanks."

"I'll tell Detective Sanders you've been informed about your brother." Mac walked him to the door. "You should be hearing from someone in the police department in a day or so."

Mac shut the door and leaned against it. Tears threatened to spill over onto her cheeks. Sometimes this job could be pretty awful.

"I wonder how Detective Sanders will feel about us being

officially on the case." Miss P picked up the mug of untouched coffee.

"We've worked together before. He'll be fine." Mac shrugged into her coat and pulled it tight against the sudden chill of uncertainty. At least she prayed he'd be okay. She'd find out soon enough. "Tell Sam I'll see her tomorrow."

CHAPTER 9

The sugary smells of ice cream, the sauces, and fresh fruit mixed with ozone from the refrigeration units hit Jake as soon as he opened the door to the Main Street Creamery. The corners of his mouth turned up in a grin.

He strolled over to study the illustrations of their elaborate milkshakes. Which one should they order? He'd let Mac choose.

"Hi." A warm arm circled his waist.

He turned to kiss her. Whoa. Zoe pressed up against him, and he took a brisk step away. Time to set her straight. "Don't do that again."

"I'm sorry." She raised a hand to her cheek as if he'd slapped her. "I thought we were friends."

"We are, but that crosses a line with me."

"I get it." She gave him a wan smile and walked away.

Why did he feel like such a heel?

Mac swung through the door and greeted Zoe. When she got to him, she gave him a brief kiss. "What's up with Zoe? I asked her to join us for ice cream, and she burst into tears. Did something happen?"

"Let's order and sit down." A stone settled in his stomach. The last thing he wanted was to talk to Mac about another woman, but what could he do?

They took a booth in the back, and Jake reached for Mac's hand across the table.

"You're scaring me, Jake Sanders. What's going on?"

He expelled a breath and raised his eyes to hers. "This afternoon, Zoe showed up at my office to tell me she got into the police academy."

"Great." Mac sat back. "She told us at lunch she was trying for it."

"Yeah, well." He scrubbed a hand through his hair. "That's not all. She gave me a big hug and kissed me on the lips."

"She did what?"

Jake glanced around and motioned for her to lower her voice. "I didn't kiss her back and pushed her away."

"I should hope so. And when were you going to tell me about her visit?" Mac pinned her crossed arms over her chest.

"I got busy and figured I'd tell you tonight. But there's more."

"Do tell."

Sweat trickled down his neck. "Just before you got here, she came up to me while I was looking at the menu and put her arm around my waist." Was steam rising off his girlfriend? "I pushed her away and told her never to do that again."

"And I invited her to have ice cream with us." Mac leaned forward, fists clenched. "If I'd known, I'd have given her something to cry about."

The waitress came over with their S'Mores milkshake, chocolate and marshmallow cream overflowing a large mug sitting on a saucer. "Enjoy."

Jake pulled it toward him and took a tentative bite. "Mac, this is so good. Let's just forget her and eat our ice cream." She turned her head away. How could he get her mind off Zoe and back on them? "The boss talked to me about a promotion."

She gave a distracted nod.

"It would mean more money." He touched her hand. "For us."

"What would you be doing?"

"Detective Sergeant. I'd oversee the detectives. We haven't had one for a few months, and the Chief is feeling overwhelmed trying to manage the detectives and do everything else he has to do."

"So, you wouldn't be actively involved in the cases?" She interlaced her fingers with his. "Is that what you want?"

Her intense chestnut-colored eyes held the same doubt he wrestled with himself.

"I don't know." He sighed.

"I'd miss the action part, the doing. I think you would too." She took his hands in hers. "But it's your decision, and I'm okay either way. I love you."

"I love you more." He raised her hand to his lips and pressed an ice cream kiss into her palm.

"You big lug." She laughed and grabbed some napkins to wipe her hand. He grinned. "We talked to a witness this afternoon."

"A witness?" Her gaze snapped back his way. "Did you learn anything?"

"Not much we didn't already know." He offered her a spoon. "Except our killer could be a woman."

Mac stopped midway to her mouth with a dripping spoonful of ice cream, chocolate syrup, and marshmallow. "You're kidding."

"Eat your ice cream before it ends up on the table." Jake

chuckled. "I'll tell you the details." He told her about the interview as he watched her take bite after bite of the gooey milkshake. When he finished, he dipped his spoon in for one last bite. "Too bad we're not working on this case together. I could get used to coming here for consultations."

"About that." Mac lowered her eyes and took a sip of water.

The hair on the back of his neck stood up. "What?"

"It seems we are working the case together."

"How so?"

"Hank Young, Vic's uncle, hired us this afternoon to find the memorabilia stolen from the time capsule."

"And when were you going to tell me?"

Mac shot him a frosty look. "I got busy and figured I'd tell you tonight."

Ouch. Jake felt the sting of her words right in the middle of his forehead. He held up his hands. "Touché."

A shadow fell on their table. "How is, or should I say was, your ice cream?" Queenie, the owner of the shop, leaned down for a hug. "Haven't seen you two here in a while."

"Great. Can you sit for a minute?" Mac patted the bench next to her.

The plump woman cast a critical eye around her store. "I think they can manage without me for a second." She squeezed in beside Mac. "Oof. Either these booths have gotten smaller, or I've put on a few pounds."

"Must be the booths." Jake patted his stomach. "I noticed it too."

"I may have to do something about that. Can't have people eating ice cream in a cramped booth."

"Speaking of business," Mac said. "Have you heard anything about the Tilted Skillet closing because the rent is being raised?"

Queenie gave Mac an are-you-for-real look. "No way. That

place is solid. Everybody's rent is going up." She tapped her elegant nails on the tabletop. "Even here. We're fine, but I don't know about next door. I heard she got herself in deep to get up and running."

"Is that why the store at the end is empty?"

"It won't be for long." The ice cream store owner's face lit up. "Do you remember David Rush? He's an artist who grew up here."

"I do," Mac said. "Didn't he move to New York or somewhere?"

"He did and became all famous and stuff." Queenie grinned. "He's opening a gallery in the space."

"Who owns this building?" Jake expected to hear the name of the bank on the corner of the building.

"Some investment firm in St. Louis."

"Not Missouri Savings and Loan?"

"No. They're renters. Just like me." She slid out of the booth. "Although we do take our rent to them every month. I guess the investment firm has an account with them."

"You can't pay your rent online?" Mac asked.

"That's how it was set up in the beginning." Queenie nodded to an employee behind the counter. "I need to go. Nice to see you guys. Come again soon."

Jake moved from his side of the booth to sit next to Mac so he could take in the interior of the shop. No nearby tables and everyone seemed engrossed in their own conversations. He placed a casual arm along the back of the booth.

"You're making me nervous again," Mac said just loud enough for him to hear.

"Something about what Queenie told us plucked one of my detective nerves." He rubbed his nose. "I need to do some research before I say anything more."

"You think there's something shady with the bank?"

"Not the bank. The so-called investment firm." He scooted out of the booth and held out a hand for Mac. "Let's get out of here."

CHAPTER 10

Sam squeezed her eyes shut. The morning pot of coffee Alan made for her smelled foul. She poured it down the sink and heated a mug of water for tea. Whatever bean he used, she'd tell him never again.

Killer, their golden doodle, trotted into the kitchen and grinned up at her.

"Not now, dog. I've got a splitting headache." She moved him aside to get to the toaster. She needed food but couldn't stomach the thought of eggs and bacon. Toast and tea would have to do for now.

Killer watched her from a corner in the kitchen, and when she took a seat at the table, he sauntered over to lean against her leg.

She dropped her hand to his head and began to stroke his fine, wavy hair. A tear drop plopped from her chin onto her plate. Next thing she knew, she was on the floor, her arms encircling her dog's neck and her face buried in his soft coat. "What's wrong with me? Am I having a breakdown?" She raised her head and swiped at her eyes. "Nothing's changed. Everything's good. Even at work. We have a client coming today." She placed her hands around Killer's face and brought it in line with her own. "So why am I crying?"

Killer licked her nose.

Sam laughed and wiped her face. "I can always count on you for a kiss." She scrambled to her feet and regained her seat. "Thanks, pup. I feel better now."

But the mood swings worried her. They'd been happening ever since her mother left right before Christmas. She drained her tea and took her cup to the sink. Gray clouds scuttled by outside. Did the lack of sunshine have something to do with it?

Pushing off the kitchen counter, Sam marched to her bedroom, determined to get a handle on her emotions. But after a button popped off her favorite blouse and she ran out of conditioner and her mascara clumped, it was all she could do not to hurl something breakable at the wall.

She threw herself on her bed. "Lord, I can't do this."

"Yes you can," A soft voice deep inside answered. "With My help."

Sam lay still. "Thanks for reminding me." She started over and got ready for work.

A quick goodbye to Killer and she was on the road. She should be at the office an hour before Mr. Young and would have time to prepare. Sam punched a number on her cellphone.

"Good morning, partner." Mac's voice sounded along with road noise over Sam's speakers.

"Just wanted to see if you were on your way in, and it sounds like you are."

"Yep. Have you talked to Jake this morning?"

"No." Uneasiness spiced with irritation sparked through her. Why did Mac do this to her? Why not just tell her the bad news without making her feel anxious? "What's going on?"

"Nothing. I told him about our new client last night and about our meeting this morning. I thought he might try to get himself invited."

"Is that all? I thought you were going to tell me something bad my brother had done."

"Sorry. I didn't mean to upset you. Why don't we talk more when you get here."

"Sure." Sam did a mental head slap. She was not getting off to a good start.

At the office, she paused on the porch. *Lord, be with me.* She took a deep breath and adjusted her smile. "Hi, guys."

Mac and Miss P stood by the side window, heads bent in conversation. They popped apart when Sam walked in, and she couldn't help getting the impression they were talking about her.

"I made you some special tea, Samantha. It's wonderful for stress and anxiety." Miss P hurried into the kitchen area.

"I brought your desk chair out to the table, so you'd have a more comfortable place to sit." Mac took Sam's coat and hung it up.

Sam bit her lip to keep from screaming.

"Stop." She slammed her purse down on the table. "Just stop. I know I've been moody lately, but you're treating me like I'm crazy."

"No, dear." Miss P set a cup and saucer in front of her. "We're treating you like your pregnant."

Sam collapsed into her desk chair and gaped at her two friends. She placed a hand on her abdomen. Could that be it?

"Close your mouth, dear, it's very unbecoming."

A giggle bubbled up in her throat that soon became a full-throated, tears-streaming-down-her-face laugh. She was going to have a baby. That explained everything. She wiped her eyes with a napkin and gave her partners a big smile. "Thank you."

"Don't thank us quite yet. We could be wrong." Miss P looked pointedly at her watch. "I believe you might want to repair your mascara before Mr. Young arrives, and we took the liberty of leaving a test kit in the restroom."

A peace descended over Sam. She'd take the test, but in her spirit, she knew her friends were right. This time, her hand was steady and her make-up flawless.

And the test was positive.

Mac knew the moment her friend reentered the room—Miss P had been right. Her heart filled with joy touched with uncertainty. What would happen to their partnership? Maybe Sam would decide to be a stay-at-home mom.

Mac didn't think she could do this job without her. She didn't want to do it without her. But for now, she needed to push those concerns aside. They had a client arriving any minute.

As the hands of the clock on the wall moved to nine, the door opened on a trim man with a full head of silver hair and a mustache to match. A cold wind followed him in and raced around, ruffling anything lightweight.

"Good morning, ladies." He closed the door and pulled his gloves off. "Looks like snow out there. I'm Hank Young."

"Mr. Young, I'm Mackenzie Love." She shook his hand.

An aura of power surrounded him—like he was used to being in charge, getting his way. She'd met men like him before, and they always had the same effect on her. They made her bristle. Between Sam's hormone swings and her push back to being told what to do, this could be an interesting meeting. Thank God for Miss P.

"Come in. Let me introduce you."

He strode ahead of her and wrapped Miss P in a bear hug. "Miss Freebody, so good to see you after all these years." After a moment, he stepped back. "You haven't changed a bit. Still as lovely as ever."

"And you're still as full of malarkey as ever, Henry Young." Miss P peered at him over her glasses. "Have a seat, sir."

"Yes, ma'am." A flash of irritation passed over his face before he laughed and pulled out a chair at the conference table.

He looked across at Sam. "You must be Samantha Majors." He stood and leaned across to shake her hand. "Glad to meet you."

Sam nodded at him.

Mac knew she needed to take control of the meeting or Young would. She folded her hands on her notepad. "Mr. Young. How can we help you?"

"Like I said on the phone, I want you to recover the contents of the time capsule." He withdrew a folded piece of paper from his pocket. "I was able to find this in the files. I think it's a complete list of what was inside." He scooted it to Mac.

PLANS FROM CITY COUNCIL for the future of Washington

Master parks plan

Newspaper

Essays from school children

Best three drawings of My Hometown from high school children

Film made of building of time capsule

Commemorative silver dollar

Photos of town and groups

"Would you make a few copies of this?" Mac passed it to Miss P. "While she's doing that, tell us why you think someone broke into the capsule and what among the items on the list was worth stealing?"

"Even before I saw the list, I couldn't wrap my mind around it." He ran a hand down his face. "Once I saw it, I was still in the dark. All I know is I'm director of parks and recreation, and my job is to get the stuff back."

"It would help us track the items on the list down if we had some idea of why they were stolen in the first place."

Miss P returned and handed Mac the original list. She gave Sam and Hank Young each a copy and kept one for herself.

"We'll study this and see if we can come up with any ideas. In the meantime, Mr. Young, please try to find out anything more you can about the individual articles placed in the time capsule."

"We haven't discussed your rate." He took out his checkbook. "How much do you want up front?"

Mac kept her eyes on her notes. Money before they start a job? Did other firms do that?

She glanced at Sam, who was staring intently at her computer. "Mrs. Majors handles our finances. I'll let you talk to her." Sorry, partner. She rose and shook his hand once more. "You should be hearing from us in a few days. Does that seem reasonable?"

"Yes. Thank you."

In her office, Mac pulled up a blank document on her computer and entered the list of items from the time capsule. At first glance, the only thing of value might be the commemorative half dollar. She needed more information. The historic society in town came to mind, and she knew just who to call.

"Mackenzie, what can I help you with this time?" Mrs. White's excited voice answered on the second ring.

"I'm curious about the 1989 time capsule commemorative half dollar. Do you know anything about it?"

"Oh my, yes." Her tone filled with suspense. "What a bizarre story. Meet me at the historic society, and I'll tell you all about it."

CHAPTER 11

For the third time that morning, Jake stopped himself before putting through a call to the bank manager of Missouri Savings and Loan. He didn't have time to run down an investment firm right now. He had a murder to solve. Not to mention destruction of public property and theft.

So why did he keep hearing this nagging voice inside telling him the two lines of inquiry were related? What could a shady business possibly have to do with what else was going on? Unless something inside the time capsule would benefit or hurt their bottom line. He ran a hand down his face. Now he was talking fairytales.

He stretched and walked down the corridor to the break room. Vic Young handed him a fresh mug of coffee.

"Anything new?"

"Nothing." Jake blew on the liquid before hazarding a sip. "We need to know what was inside the capsule."

"That's my priority today. My uncle is director of parks and recreation. I'll get in touch with him."

"We also need to go talk to Tim Koenig about his brother, Freddy."

"I can do that after I get ahold of Hank."

"No. I need you here. I'll send Walker." Jake gave the coffee in his mug a gentle swirl. "We need some idea about motive. So far, we've got nada." Vic's mention of his uncle reminded him what Mac said last night. His next call would be to his girlfriend. "Stick around. We'll talk later."

He got an automatic can-I-call-you-later text from Mac. Which meant she was busy. Probably meeting with Young right now. He could show up at their office and get a chance to talk to the guy too. But Mac would be spitting mad. Not to mention his sister. She'd been moody lately.

When his phone rang, he snatched it up, certain it was Mac. "Hi, sweetheart." The pause on the other end told him he goofed.

"Detective Sanders?" the female voice asked.

"Yes, ma'am. Sorry. I thought you were someone else." Thank God he wasn't on FaceTime because his face was red hot.

"No problem. This is Queenie from the Creamery."

Jake pulled a pad of paper over and grabbed a pen. "Good morning, Queenie."

"After our talk last night, I got to wondering about my lease, so I dug it out of my files. You seemed so interested I thought you might want to know the name of the investment company that owns the building."

"Thanks for going to all the trouble."

"You better hold your thanks, Detective, because I was wrong. The owners of the building are local, a group of investors called Fischer, Baker, and Young."

Jake's stomach clenched. "Do you have first names?"

"Only initials. G. Fischer, O. Baker, and H. Young, but I

think you and me know who they are. I hope this helps answer any questions you have."

"You've been a great help, Queenie. Thanks." Jake pressed End and filled in the names after the initials. Brandon Fischer, Owen Baker, and Henry Young. Alarms echoed inside his head. The question was—why?

He tried Mac's number again and got the same result. Ten o'clock. Her meeting with Mr. Young should be over by now. He grabbed his coat and hat. If they got mad, too bad. His murder case trumped her case. Whatever it was.

His phone rang, and he dug it out of his pocket. He checked before answering this time. "Where have you been? I've been calling you all morning." He plopped into his chair. "All I got were those stupid texts."

"Don't take that tone with me, Jake Sanders. I don't work for you."

He pinched the bridge of his nose and counted to ten. "Sorry. This case is ..."

"Maybe this will make you feel better. I've learned something this morning that might help us both."

"What?"

"Mr. Young brought us a list of the contents of the time capsule. I'm emailing it to you now."

Jake opened his computer. "I've got it." He scanned the list and went back over it more carefully. The hope that raised his spirits a moment ago flickered and died. "Do you see anything here worth killing for?"

"The only thing I wondered about was the commemorative coin. I'm on my way to see Mrs. White at the historic society now. She said there's a story behind it. I'll let you know as soon as I find out."

"It could be nothing."

"Or it could be the key to why everything happened."

A smile lifted the corners of his mouth. That's what he liked about them as a couple. When one was down, the other encouraged. They worked well together.

"Talk to you later. I'll study this list some more and see if I can't come up with any other ideas." He pressed Print and shrugged out of his coat.

Something on the list moved at the edges of his reason. Whenever he pivoted to grab the idea, it turned to smoke. Maybe if he stared at the list long enough. Or another pair of eyes might help.

He rolled his chair to his door and called down the hall. "Vic. You busy?"

"What do you need? I've been trying to get my uncle all morning."

"Never mind. We've got the list." Jake handed him a copy. "Sit. What do you see?"

Vic scanned the page. "The only thing that seems like it could be interesting is the half dollar. Where you'd get this?"

"Mac had a meeting with your uncle this morning, and he gave it to her." Jake scratched his chin. "Something on this list is worth killing for. What aren't we seeing?" He tossed the paper onto his desk—before he tore it into little pieces.

"Okay." Vic rubbed the back of his neck. "Let's take each one. Who would be interested in plans for the city?"

"The people who live here? The businesses?" Jake pushed up in his chair. His insides hummed like they did when he was about to make a breakthrough on a case. "Investors. The same with the parks plans." He grabbed the paper off his desk. "They'd pay big money to know what property to buy and sell to the city later for a profit."

"What made you think of investors?"

"A conversation I had earlier with Queenie, the owner of Main Street Creamery. I'll give you the whole story later." He texted the names of the men Queenie had given him to Vic. "In the meantime, we need to take a closer look at these guys. Your uncle is on the list. Is that a problem for you?"

"No. We're not close. My dad and him never got along." A line formed across Vic's forehead. "You think they may have something to do with all this?"

"Maybe. Could be all of them. Could be one of them. Or none of them." Jake removed his coat from his chair and hung it back on the rack along with his hat. "That's what we need to find out."

CHAPTER 12

Anticipation sparked every nerve as Mackenzie neared the Washington Historical Society Museum at Fourth and Market. Mrs. White helped solve two of their previous cases. Why not a third?

The petite woman greeted Mac at the door with a broad smile. "I've been waiting for you. Follow me." She stopped and threw up her hands. "Where are my manners? Let me take your coat, my dear. Would you like a bottled water? I'm afraid that's all we allow in the museum proper."

"I'm fine." Mac followed Mrs. White's bustling figure to an office on the right. She was about to enter when the woman hurried toward her.

"No, no. I want to begin out here. This way please." She led Mac to a section of the museum that contained photos and exhibits displayed according to decades. "Let's examine what we have around the period the time capsule was established in Rennick Park."

Together they read through newspaper articles about the

sesquicentennial celebration, studied photos of how Washington looked in 1989, and examined artifacts from that time. Mrs. White kept up a running commentary of details she knew and that weren't present in any of the exhibits.

The only thing Mac found of interest was a list of Time Capsule Committee members, but from their pictures, she was sure many of them were dead by now. She turned her back on the display. Across the narrow room photos from another era caught her eye. Were those her parents? She crossed to a picture of a parade and leaned close.

"Those are from around 2015, Mackenzie." Mrs. White touched her arm. "Now that we've learned some background, I have something far more interesting to show you in my office."

Mac tore her eyes from the photo with a promise to herself to come back later and examine it more thoroughly. Along with the others on the wall. Those pictures would have been taken around the time of their deaths. She glanced back over her shoulder before entering Mrs. White's office.

"Have a seat, my dear." The plump white-haired woman closed and locked the door behind her. She flipped the overhead light on and moved quickly around the room, closing the blinds on all the windows. "That's better."

Better for what? Anticipation rippled through her. What was the historian about to reveal to her?

"You mentioned an interest in the contents of the time capsule." Mrs. White opened two doors of a storage cabinet situated under the windows.

Inside stood a sturdy safe. She blocked Mac's view for a moment.

"Yes. I brought the list with me hoping you could tell me more details about some of the items." At the distinct sound of a locking mechanism, Mac's pulse quickened. "On the phone, you said something about a strange story behind the commemorative half dollar. I'm most interested in that."

"As you should be, my dear." The historian placed a clear bag on the blotter on her desk. "Let me settle myself, and I'll explain."

The bag held something round and flat with a silver glint. Mac itched to open it.

"Don't touch." Mrs. White pulled out two pairs of white cotton gloves from a drawer. "Not until you put these on. The oil from our hands will tarnish it."

Mac held her breath as the woman opened the bag and tipped the coin onto a white cloth she'd spread between them.

"Before you handle it, do not hold it too close to your face for long. Use this magnifying glass to see details. It's a very peculiar ... Well, I won't say anything more. I'll let you discover its oddities on your own." She sat back.

Mac scooted close to the desk and pulled the cloth near to her. The half dollar gleamed as if it was newly minted. The etching of President Kennedy, 1989, and the words 'Liberty' and 'In God We Trust' stood out sharp and clear.

"The bank ordered rolls of these to give to the citizens in commemoration of the sesquicentennial. It was a grand gesture," the historian said.

"It's beautiful. What's it worth in today's market?"

"A normal 1989 half dollar is worth anywhere from three to one hundred dollars. Depending on what someone is willing to pay for it."

Mac lifted her gaze to her. That was hardly a king's ransom and certainly not worth killing for.

"But this isn't a normal coin." Mrs. White lifted an eyebrow at her. "Turn it over."

Mac did as she was told. At first, she didn't see the problem. On the back, 'United States of America' arced across the top with 'E Pluribus Unum' and an eagle with spread wings and olive branches. But the words under the eagle said 'Quarter Dollar.'

"They put the back of a quarter on the half dollar." Mac gripped the magnifying glass as her heart beat faster.

"Exactly." Mrs. White grinned at Mac as if she'd passed a final exam. "It's called a mule coin, and collectors pay a lot of money for them. In this case, about two hundred thousand dollars."

Mac whistled. "Why so much?"

"When the bank opened the roll and realized what had happened, they packed the lot up and sent them back." Mrs. White polished the coin and replaced it in its bag. "However, five coins had been given out. They appealed to the public to bring them in, saying they weren't legal tender. Four people did, but one didn't. The bank let us keep one of the ones returned." She placed it in the safe and closed the door. "Another went into the time capsule. The other two were destroyed."

"How many people knew about the coins?"

"I guess the bank knew they existed, but no one knew we received one except the woman in charge of memorabilia and us. We kept it very hush-hush. I think only the committee knew about the time capsule."

"And the other coin?"

"We never knew. The bank's records were lost." Mrs. White removed her gloves and put out her hand for the ones Mac was wearing. "But one was sold at auction a few years later for fifteen thousand dollars."

"I thought you said two hundred thousand."

"I did. The coin disappeared until it resurfaced at auction two years ago where it sold for two hundred thousand." Mrs.

White peered at her. "I must ask you not to divulge the existence of the half dollar at the museum. Please."

"I won't."

"I'm sure you can understand why, given its value." The historian sighed. "I keep trying to get my superior to put it in a safe deposit box at the bank, but for some reason, she won't."

"Thank you for trusting me and showing me the coin." Mac pushed to her feet. "I'll tell my partners the story about the coin, but not about actually seeing one in person."

"Did you want me to look at the rest of the list?"

Mac hesitated. What would be gained? On the other hand, what would she lose? She unfolded the paper and placed it in the woman's outstretched hand.

"This takes me back." The woman's pudgy cheeks lifted in a smile. "I was a young history teacher at the time. I judged the drawings for the contest."

"What contest?" Mac regained her seat.

"The drawing contest." Mrs. White's gaze unfocused as if into the past. "The high school students entered artwork representing the town of Washington, and we chose three for the time capsule. Of course, David Rush's piece was one of the three."

"David Rush. Queenie was talking about him the other day."

"He left here for somewhere out east ..." Mrs. White waved a hand around. "And became famous. Supposedly he's back in town to open a gallery."

"He's renting the empty spot by the creamery."

"How wonderful. He showed remarkable talent as a young man, and I'm told he's a very accomplished artist. Just what this town needs."

"What about the other two drawings? Do you remember who did those?"

"No. I'm sorry." Mrs. White handed the list back to Mac. "I suppose the early drawing by David would be worth a fair sum today. Since he's made such a name for himself."

"I guess so." Mac shouldered her purse. She knew nothing about art. Could possessing a high school sketch of a now famous artist be enough incentive to kill? She doubted it, but getting hold of the silver dollar ...

CHAPTER 13

J ake stared at the piece of paper in front of him. Brandon
Fischer, Owen Baker, and Henry Young. Three upstanding
men of the community, and he was about to treat them as
if they were suspects in a murder. Sweat beaded on his upper
lip. He could be making the biggest mistake of his career.

"I'll connect with my uncle." Vic scrawled something on
the notepad in front of him. "I can talk to him about the list,
ask him what he knows about each item, and see what he has
to say about the investor group he's a part of."

"Hang on. Let's think about this." His job wasn't the only
one on the line. What about Vic?

"What's to think about? We're only going to ask a few
questions."

"Yeah, well, your uncle is only one of them. Remember the
Chief's brother is another member of the group. How do you
propose we approach him?"

"Good question." Vic sat back in his chair. "Maybe we need
to take our suspicions to the boss and ask him what to do?"

Jake knew that was the right thing to do, but his left eye

DEBORAH SPRINKLE

developed a twitch at the thought. Chief Baker had enough on his plate with running the department and his niece, Ivy, serving her two-year sentence at a mental health facility.

The Chief tended to take on responsibility for everything that went wrong in Washington and in his family. Jake wasn't keen on adding to his burden. Especially since this brother was Ivy's father.

"I could speak to him if you want." Vic shifted in his chair.

"No." He sighed. "We'll both go." Jake stuffed the list of names into the file and pushed to his feet.

Before they could leave, Detective Walker appeared at Jake's door. "I talked to Tim Koenig like you asked, but he wasn't much help. Freddy, his brother, had been living in St. Louis. He had no idea who his friends were or his dentist." The big man shrugged. "I got DNA from him, but that's it. I sent it to the lab. Should hear something in about a week."

"I didn't expect much." Jake shook his head. "Maybe the sample will be enough. If I need anything more, I'll let you know."

When Jake and Vic got to the Chief's open door, he looked up and narrowed his gaze at them. "What's the problem?"

"No problem—yet." Jake pinched the bridge of his nose.

"Sit." The Chief folded his hands on the desk. "Out with it."

"We're investigating this theft and homicide at the park."

"I read the reports."

"Vic and I have been trying to figure out a motive. What could be so valuable in the time capsule that it was worth killing for."

The Chief nodded. "Logical."

"Here's a list of objects put in the capsule." Jake handed a copy to Chief Baker. "Vic and I started going through it item by item." He cut his eyes to his fellow detective. Between them, they related to the Chief their morning conversation.

"When we saw your brother was one of the investors, we decided to talk to you first before pursuing this any further, sir," Vic said.

Weariness flashed across the Chief's face before it hardened into his stony visage once more. "I'll talk to him. If he's involved in any of this, I'll find out. You two take the others."

"Do you think that's wise, sir? Conflict of interest and all?"

"Who was going to speak to your uncle, Detective Young?"

"I was, sir." Color splotched Vic's cheeks.

"I'll be careful how I approach him, and if there's any further questioning that needs to be done, one of you can be in charge." The Chief picked up his phone, signaling the meeting was over. "I expect the same from you, Detective."

"Yes, sir."

That left Brandon Fischer, Mr. Fischer's son, for Jake to interview. The same Brandon Fischer who was trustee to Rosa Lombardi's estate. Somehow he couldn't see Fischer mixed up in theft and murder, but he'd been wrong about people before.

As they left the Chief's office, Vic put out a hand to stop Jake. "I'll get in touch with Hank today and get back to you."

"I'll speak to Fischer. Talk later." He continued down the hall to his office, his mind wrestling with how best to approach Brandon.

Maybe he should visit Brandon's father first on the pretense of seeing what the older man remembered about the time capsule? He had an established relationship with the elder Mr. Fischer. But how could he bring Brandon in on the conversation?

"Boy, you must have something heavy on your mind. I've been calling your name, and you've ignored me every time."

Brandon Fischer materialized before him, and it took every ounce of training and experience Jake had to turn his astonishment into a welcoming smile. *Okay, Lord, I guess we're going with the direct approach. I'm counting on You to give me the right words here.*

"I was just coming to see you." Jake studied the man's face for any reaction. Nothing, besides the expected amused surprise.

"You found me out." Brandon put his hands together in front of himself. "Yes, officer, I did assist that squirrel in committing suicide on Fifth Street this morning."

Jake barked a laugh. "I never heard hitting a squirrel described that way." He ushered Fischer into his office. "Sit down for a minute. I want to pick your brain."

"Okay." He grinned at Jake and took a gulp of his bottled water.

Jake made a show of opening his file and studying what was written there.

"What's going on, Jake?"

"I'm kind of stumped." He held up the list of items from the time capsule. "You've heard about the theft and homicide?"

"Sure. It's all the town's talking about." Brandon shook his head. "Terrible thing. Can't figure it out."

"Well, I've got a list of what was inside the capsule, but I can't figure out why anyone would break it open for this." Jake thumped the paper with his fingers. "Much less kill for it."

"Can I see it?"

Jake scrunched his face together. "I'm not sure I should, but I guess it's okay since I'm kind of bringing you in on a consulting basis." He handed the paper to Fischer and watched as he read through it. No shaking hands or tensing of the jaw.

He gave the list back to Jake. "The only thing I see is the half-dollar. Maybe. And it wouldn't be much unless there was something strange about it."

"Yeah." Jake rubbed his chin. "I wondered about the plans for the city."

"What about them?"

"Would they be worth something to an investor?" Jake raised his eyes to Fischer's.

"Why are you asking me that?" Brandon scooted his chair back a fraction.

"Aren't you in an investor's group with Owen Baker and Henry Young?" Jake shrugged. "I thought you might have some insight. You know, as an investor."

"Oh, that." Brandon's shoulders relaxed. "I went in with them to buy a couple of buildings at the beginning of the Covid pandemic, but I've gotten out of the investor game." He waved a hand in the air. "I don't have the necessary kind of money lying around."

"I'd still be interested in what you think about my idea."

Fischer scooted closer. "Let me see the list again." He pulled on his lip as he stared at the piece of paper once more. "It could be worth something to a high stakes investor who wanted to make a killing. Sorry, poor choice of words."

"Do you know any of those?"

Something flitted across Fischer's face before he could hide it away. "Let me think about it and get back to you." He stood.

Jake's nose quivered. A name had flashed into Brandon Fisher's mind, but Jake had learned to be patient. Fischer would tell him when he was ready.

"Thanks for putting up with my questions, Brandon, and I'd appreciate it if you'd keep our meeting to yourself." Jake gave his hand a squeeze as they shook.

"Got it," he said with a nervous laugh. "My lips are sealed. I'm sorry I couldn't be of more help, Detective."

Jake waited for the door to close.

"Oh, but you were, my friend. You just don't know it yet. And you'll be even more help in the future."

CHAPTER 14

S now fell in heavy wet flakes as Mackenzie left the museum and headed for her sedan. A car had come and gone since she'd been inside, and tire tracks marred the blanket of white. Not only that, but depressions like footprints surrounded her vehicle. A shiver ran through her that had nothing to do with being cold. Someone had inspected her vehicle.

She knelt and peered under her car. "If anyone's looking, they'll think I'm crazy, but too bad."

"Is something wrong?"

Mac popped to her feet, her heart pounding in her chest. Mrs. White stood a few feet away, a perplexed look on her face.

"No, no. I dropped my keys." Mac brushed snow from her knees. "I'm fine."

"Well, I'm glad I caught you." The historian handed Mac a file. "I found this after you left. It contains the names of the time capsule committee members, and I believe, everyone else involved with the celebration."

"Thank you."

"Oh dear. It looks as if you have a flat. Shall I call someone?"

Mac's eyes darted to her front left tire. She could make out the slash from where she stood, and her throat constricted, making it hard to speak. "No, thank you." She took a breath. "I'll get someone to come get me and take care of it in the morning if that's okay."

"Of course, my dear. Why don't you come inside to wait?"

Mac pressed one on her phone for Jake. "I need you to come pick me up."

"What's wrong?"

"I'll tell you when you get here. I'm at the Historic Museum."

"You're a block from the precinct. Just walk over."

Mac became aware of Mrs. White hovering nearby. "Jake, I really need you to come get me."

He must have finally picked up on the urgency in her voice.

"I'll be there in five."

As Jake's police-issued SUV pulled up, Mac said good-bye to Mrs. White once more. Instead of hopping in, she went around to his window. "I've got something to show you."

"What's going on?"

"When I came out, I could see someone had been messing with my car."

"How could you tell?"

"They left prints in the snow." In the last twenty minutes, the footprints had almost filled with new snow. "Believe me, they were there."

"I see them." Jake studied the snow cover around her car. "What do you think he was looking for?"

"I have no idea but look what he did." She pointed to her tire, and sudden anger surged through her. "I just got these."

"I'm glad you didn't walk over to the station." Jake

squatted by the damaged tire. "Sometimes a guy will do this to isolate his victim. He could have grabbed you while you were on your way to me." He rose and pulled Mac into his arms. "Thank God you insisted I come here."

"What would somebody want with me?" She pushed away from him and began to pace.

Some of the anxiety from last fall surfaced inside her. A case of mistaken identity led to her kidnapping, and she came close to a break down. She prayed this had nothing to do with what happened then.

"Mackenzie. I know what you're thinking." Jake stepped in front of her. "Stop."

She raised her eyes to his strong face, and peace washed over her. That part of her life was over, and the people responsible were in prison. She'd made it through with the help of friends and family. *Thank You, Lord.*

"Let's go. I've got a lot to tell you." She climbed into the SUV. "I think I've found the motive for the theft and killing."

"Me too." Jake settled behind the wheel.

"You already know about the coin?" She cringed at the sharp tone in her voice. "I mean, I was hoping to surprise you."

"You did." He cut his eyes to her. "I wasn't talking about any coin."

"What were you talking about?"

"The plans for the city." Jake pulled into his parking space and shut off his car. He held up a hand. "Wait till we get to my office, and I'll explain."

Plans for the city? She followed him up the stairs in the Public Safety Building. How could the plans possibly be worth as much as the mule half-dollar? As she dropped into a chair in front of Jake's desk, the door opened.

"Sorry." Detective Young stopped short. "Didn't know you had company. Hi, Mac."

Jake motioned him in. "I was about to tell Mac our theory about motive and about my interview with Brandon Fischer."

"I'd like to hear about Fischer and thought I'd let you know how it went with my uncle." Vic slid into the chair next to Mac.

The glint in Vic's eyes made Mac pull her notepad from her purse. Maybe the guys were on to something.

"What did your uncle have to say?" Jake asked.

"Whoa." Mac flipped a hand in the air. "I need some background first. Why are you talking to Henry and Brandon in the first place?"

"It all started with a call I got from Queenie." Jake rubbed his eyes. Was that only this morning? It seemed like days ago. "She phoned to tell me who the investors are who own the building."

"Brandon Fischer, Owen Baker, and my uncle, Henry Young." Vic tapped the screen of his phone. "I interviewed my uncle, Jake talked to Brandon, and we're leaving Owen to the Chief."

"But how does this tie in with the time capsule theft and the murder?"

"That's where the plans for Washington come in." Jake removed the list of items stolen from the capsule and placed it on his desk so Mac could see it.

As he explained their theory to Mac, his excitement grew. He was sure they were on to something. Once he had the name of the high-stakes investor, it would a done deal. And he already had a good idea who it would be.

"All we need is a name." Jake tapped the list.

"What if it's none of these three men?" Mac asked.

"We'll keep looking. There can't be that many investors

interested in Washington, Missouri." Jake leaned on his desk. "Besides, it's a place to start. Let me tell you what I learned from Brandon Fischer." He opened the file once more. "Fischer says he did go in with the other two to buy a couple properties but has since gotten out of the game."

"Did you believe him?" Vic pulled on his earlobe.

"Yeah. I asked him what he thought about someone going after the plans, and he said it would have to be a high-stakes investor. I asked him if he knew any."

"What did he say?"

"He said no, but the look on his face told a different story." An uneasy feeling settled between Jake's shoulder blades. Should he have pushed Fischer to give him a name? "I'll interview him again in a day or so."

"Uncle Henry confirmed some of what you got from Brandon Fischer. He told me their investor group formed at the beginning of the Covid pandemic and bought a couple of buildings downtown, but they more or less disbanded after that." Vic leaned forward, his face lit with excitement. "But when I asked him to look at the list of items in the capsule—that's when it got interesting."

CHAPTER 15

Mac scooted forward in her chair. Did Vic's Uncle Henry know about the half-dollar and its value? If so, did that make him a suspect? She couldn't stand the suspense. "Come on, Vic, out with it. What happened next?"

Jake glared at her. "My office, remember, Mac?"

"Sorry." But she wasn't really. She picked at a cuticle in frustration.

"Uncle Henry—Hank—told me the list was incomplete." Vic threw a triumphant look at Jake and Mac.

It took a moment for his words to register with her. Nothing about the coin at all.

"How could he know?" Jake asked.

"Because he remembers his dad, my grandpa, telling him he gave the committee three items to put into the time capsule." Vic held up three fingers. "A German Bible the family brought with them when they settled here, an antique map of Washington from when it was first laid out as a city, and a letter his dad, my great grandfather, received fifty years earlier from the mayor of his hometown in Germany on the occasion of the centennial celebration of Washington."

Jake tossed his pen onto his desk and scrubbed his hands down his face. "So now we've got to research old Bibles, antique maps, and stamps. And no telling what else was left off the list."

"Stamps?"

"I'm assuming the letter is in its original envelope."

Mac nodded. Makes sense. Especially with letters from the homeland. But she doubted any of those things would come close to the value of the mule coin. "I've got news about the half-dollar that should make your job a lot easier."

She could tell Jake and Vic were only half listening to her until she got to the point about the half-dollar being miscast.

"What do they call it again?" Jake asked.

"A mule coin."

"Is it rare? Worth something?"

She smirked to herself. Here was where she'd get their full attention.

"The last one sold at auction for two hundred thousand dollars."

"Did you say two hundred?" Vic's head whipped up from his notes.

"Yep." She let her lips lift in a how-about-that grin.

"I think we found—you found—our motive." Jake gave a low whistle.

"You should still check out the Bible, map, and stamp angles."

"We will, but I can't imagine anything coming close to matching that number. Unless somebody else remembers putting a diamond necklace in this thing." Jake sighed. "I guess our next step is to find out who knew about the—what did you call it again?"

"It's called a mule imprint. I guess because the front side is normal, and the back is stamped with a different denomination altogether." Something Jake said scratched at her memory. "I forgot the file." Mac leaped from her chair.

"What file?"

"The one Mrs. White gave me in the parking lot. I left it at the museum." She grabbed her coat. "It's got the names of all the people who may have known what was in the time capsule. We need to get it."

"Hang on." Jake looked at his phone. "They're closed by now. We'll have to get it tomorrow when we get your flat fixed."

She dropped onto the chair again. Her slashed tire, she corrected him in her mind. "Do you think my investigation and the vandalism to my car are related?"

"Yes." Jake's blue eyes darkened. "I don't want you traveling around town on your own for a while. Call me, and I'll send a car to take you to the office. Make sure Sam goes with you wherever you go."

"Sorry, I can't." No way was she putting her pregnant friend in danger, but Sam hadn't officially told her brother yet. What should she do?

"Why not?"

Ouch. He was using his detective tone of voice with her. "Let me make a phone call, and I promise to explain." She jumped up and left the room before he could say anything more. Yanking her phone from her pocket, she punched two for Samantha.

"What is it? We're at the doctor's office."

"I'm with your brother, and he's insisting we stick together because he's concerned for my safety. I don't want to because I don't want to put you in danger, but I didn't know if I could tell him you're pregnant." Mac took a breath.

"Mackenzie, you've done it again, haven't you? I told you before, no more cases where we get shot at, knocked on the head, or in any way in fear for our lives, but you just can't seem to do it." Sam groaned. "I give you permission to tell Jake I'm pregnant. We'll discuss this later."

Before Mac could say anything more, the line went dead. She swallowed the knot in her throat, and it hurt all the way down to her stomach. "Sorry, my friend," she murmured before opening the door to Jake's office.

Inside, Vic studied his notes, head down, while Jake followed her progress across the room with a stern look. She settled herself once more in the chair and met his gaze.

"Samantha is pregnant," Mac said.

Astonishment followed by joy transformed Jake's face from a detective to the man she loved. He rushed around his desk, grabbed her into his arms, and danced around the room. "I'm going to be an uncle."

She giggled at his unbridled enthusiasm.

"Congratulations, Jake. That's awesome." Vic slapped his fellow detective on the back.

The look on Jake's face brought tears of laughter to Mac's eyes. He'd forgotten Vic was in the room.

"Thanks, Vic." His neck and face turned flaming red as he regained his composure and walked back to his chair.

"Now you understand why I will not take Samantha with me anywhere. I'm not even sure I want her at the office. Most of what she does, she could do from home."

Jake nodded. "But that leaves you without a chaperone. I'm busy, and Miss P is too fragile."

"Listen, the tire may have been an isolated incident." Mac locked eyes with Jake. "Why don't we give it a few days to see if anything else happens before talking about a companion for me?"

"I don't know." Jake pressed his lips together. "Don't you have any friends you can call on?"

"They all work or have families."

"What about your woman friend who's going to be a police officer?" Vic looked at Mac.

"You mean Zoe?" Mac stiffened.

"Yeah. The blonde. Stands about this tall." Vic stood and held his hand at eye level, a silly grin on his face.

Mac fought to keep her face neutral. The blonde who kept flirting with her boyfriend. The one she threatened to deck at the ice cream store yesterday. She glanced at Jake, who seemed to find something very interesting on his desk. "I'll think about it, Vic."

"I'm going to type up my notes." Vic turned at the doorway. "Is Sam's news public?"

"I wouldn't tell anyone yet," Mac said.

"Got it. See you later." He closed the door.

Mac knocked on Jake's desk. He smiled at her as if all was right with the world. She wanted to strangle him.

"I noticed you weren't offering an opinion about Zoe being my temporary companion, Jake Sanders." She narrowed her gaze.

"I don't think you want to hear what I have to say on the subject." He matched her look with one of his own. "And I don't feel like arguing right now."

"I won't get mad." She willed her body to remain calm and her face receptive.

"Given the situation, Zoe seems like your only option, and I think it's a good one." He closed the file on his desk. "You were friends in high school."

"Kind of." They were friends—then—but now?

"So what's the problem?"

"The problem is she's flirting with my boyfriend, you big

93

lug." She wasn't sure if she was angrier at Zoe for flirting or Jake for acting like it was nothing.

"I told you I put a stop to that. If you don't trust me, we've got a bigger problem."

The backs of her eyes stung with unshed tears. Why was she reacting like a teenager? She was a grown woman. Was it a matter of trust or her own insecurity? "I've never been in this position before." She studied her hands, folded in her lap. "Because I've never cared about someone as much as I do for you."

Jake came around his desk for the second time and pulled her into his arms. "I love you, and I always will." He lifted her chin, and his look made her stomach flip. "There is no other woman for me."

A knock sounded on his door.

Jake stepped away, trailing his hand along her waist, and a ribbon of heat twirled inside her.

Vic poked his head inside. "The Chief wants to see us."

Jake nodded, never taking his eyes off Mac.

"I'll call Zoe and ask her to join the firm on a temporary basis."

"Great," Vic said.

Mac shifted her gaze to Vic and back to Jake. At least with Zoe by her side, she could keep an eye on the blonde beauty.

CHAPTER 16

The aroma of brewing coffee wafted through the house. Mac pulled on her jeans, sweater, and a pair of wool socks against the morning chill and padded into the living room. The outside temperature hovered above freezing, and sunshine melted some of the snow from yesterday, leaving behind patches of brown grass in her yard and turning the roads into a rutted mess. A dark-colored van was parked across the street. "Never seen that one before."

She pulled her boots on and stepped out onto the porch. The morning paper lay at her feet. She stooped as if picking it up, reversed direction, and raced across the lawn toward the van. If there was no one inside, she'd feel foolish, and she prayed she wouldn't slip in the icy sludge.

The van took off, its rear end breaking loose before the tires found pavement under the slush. Mac whipped out her phone and took a series of photos. Standing in the middle of the street, frustration and anger fought for first place in her attitude. None of those would move her any closer to finding the mementos from the time capsule or help find who was stalking her.

But she'd been here before, and she didn't like it.

Her phone vibrated in her hand. "Hi, Jake."

"What's the matter?"

Did he have the same special gift Samantha did? "What makes you think anything's wrong?"

"'Hi' instead of 'good morning,' and I can tell your breathing is different. Like you've been running or something."

"You must be a detective." She snatched her paper off the porch and headed inside where she made a beeline for the coffee pot.

"I try. Are you going to tell me what happened?"

"Let me get my coffee first." She wrapped her hands around the warm mug and eased into her rocker. "I saw a strange van outside, and when I tried to get close, it took off."

"Did you get a license plate number?" He'd switched to his detective tone.

"I snapped some photos as he pulled away."

"Text those to me, and I'll get someone to look at them." He paused. "When do you need me to pick you up?"

"Zoe's coming to get me. I figured we might as well get started right away." She took a drink. "Leonard is towing my car to his shop to fix my tire. Zoe and I will go to the Historical Museum to get the file, and afterwards, past Leonard's to see how things are going."

"Sounds like you've got it covered." A note of regret sounded in Jake's voice. "Call if you need anything."

"Hopefully, I won't need you to talk me out of strangling my companion."

"You'll be fine." He chuckled. "But I'll take you to lunch."

"Sounds good. We'll talk later." Mac finished her coffee and headed for her bedroom where a cozy chair, a reading lamp, and a table sat in one corner.

A perfect spot to read her Bible and meditate when something bothered her, and she definitely had something on her mind. She wanted to clear the air with Zoe about Jake, but how could she without sounding like a petulant teenager?

Lord, I need Your help. Give me the right words at the right time. Most of all, keep my mouth closed if either the words or the timing is wrong.

And, if it's not Your will for me to say anything, help me accept that and be able to work with Zoe anyway. Amen.

But could she work with Zoe and not say anything? The more likely scenario would be she'd blurt something out the minute the woman walked in the door. She looked at the ceiling. "I'll try. I really will."

She cleaned her mug in the kitchen sink and grabbed a sweet and salty granola bar. The doorbell rang as she took the first bite. Mac struggled to chew the sticky, nutty mess in her mouth. So much for assaulting Zoe when she arrived. She'd be lucky to manage a smile. *God works in mysterious ways.*

"I can't tell you how excited and honored I am to be working with you." Zoe threw her arms around Mac and gave her a big hug. "It's like a dream come true. I know I'm going to learn so much from you."

Mac swallowed and disengaged herself from Zoe's enthusiastic embrace. "I wouldn't get too excited."

"Oh, Mac. I've heard about you and Samantha and all the amazing cases you've solved." Zoe nodded, solemnly. "You guys are good. The best."

Maybe working with Zoe wouldn't be all bad. "Let me get my coat, and we'll get started."

"Great. Where to?"

"The Washington Historic Museum."

"Great. Where's that?"

"I'll navigate." Mac held up a hand to stop Zoe's reply. "I know—great."

"I'm nervous. Sorry." She pointed to the door. "I'll warm up the car."

"Gr—fine. I'll be out in a minute." Mac forced a smile onto her face. "You want a coffee?"

"No thanks. I don't drink coffee." Zoe closed the door behind her.

"Why am I not surprised?" Mac trudged back to the kitchen. "Positive attitude, can't wait to work with me, but doesn't drink coffee." She glanced up. "Just when I think You're smoothing the way. Who doesn't drink coffee?" She filled her to-go cup and shoved her granola bar into her pocket. "I can do this." Every time she felt the urge to be ugly, she'd take a bite. She only hoped it lasted until lunch.

In the car, Mac alternated between giving Zoe directions and telling her what had happened so far. She skipped over a lot to get to why they were starting with the museum. "I came out and saw my tire had been slashed. That's when I called Jake."

"What did he think?"

"He believes I have a stalker." Mac indicated the parking lot entrance for the museum. "Pull in here."

"Do you agree?"

"Yes. Especially after what happened this morning." Mac swung her legs out of the car. "I saw a dark-colored van outside my house, and when I ran toward it, he drove away."

"Yikes."

"Yeah." Mac scanned the area. "While I'm inside, I'd like you to keep an eye out for any cars that look out of place or seem suspicious."

"You're going to have to be more specific."

"Cars that drive by slowly as if they're looking for something or someone, pass more than once or twice in a short span of time, or pull into the parking lot or across the street, stay for a little while, and leave."

"Got it."

"I won't be long." Mac studied the doors into the museum. "Probably the best place to watch would be just inside the doors. They have good windows. You'd be warm, and nobody will see you."

They crossed to the museum.

"Did you bring a notebook?" Mac should have asked her before they left.

Zoe pulled a small spiral pad from her coat pocket.

"Good. I'll retrieve the file, and we can go to our next stop."

Mac knocked on Mrs. White's office door before entering. "Good morning."

"I didn't expect to see you. The young man came and towed your car earlier today." The historian yawned and gave Mac a hug. "Forgive me. The Downtown Merchants group had their meeting here last night, and they didn't finish until ten. I had to stay to lock up." She plopped into her chair. "What can I do for you?"

"I came by to pick up the file you gave me yesterday. The one listing everyone who knew about the contents of the time capsule. I must have left it when Jake picked me up."

"Oh. I haven't seen it."

"It was right here." Mac touched the corner of the desk by the phone. "Would someone refile it?"

"I doubt it. I found it in the archives." Mrs. White searched among the papers she'd been working on and the piles of books lying about. "I don't see it. Are you sure you didn't have it with you?"

"Positive." Her mouth went dry.

CHAPTER 17

"Do you keep your office locked when you're not here?" Could the file have been thrown out accidentally? Mac surveyed the tidy room.

"Not usually, but I can't imagine why anyone would take anything from here." Mrs. White gestured to her desk.

"Can I ask for one more crazy favor?"

The older woman nodded.

"Would you text me a list of who was here last night?"

"Mackenzie, I ..." Her forehead creased as she straightened the pile of papers on her desk. "I'm concerned about you. The citizens of this town are good people. They don't go around stealing other people's property."

"Yet someone—probably one of those good citizens—hired a man to break into the time capsule, and later, killed him." Mac caught her historian friend's bright eyes in an unrelenting stare. "I'm trying to find out who that someone is."

"I'll send you the list." The older woman averted her gaze, the gleam no longer present.

"Thank you." Mac slipped out of the office and closed the door. She stood in the hall with her back to the wall.

Guilt sat like a stone in Mac's chest. She hated bursting the bubble of trust Mrs. White had in the people around her. But what choice did she have? She had a job to do, and someone kept getting in the way.

She came up behind Zoe. "Anything suspicious?"

"A red sedan drove by going north, but I didn't see it again, and a man walked his dog through the parking lot. I think it was some sort of spaniel. The man with the dog went into the house across the street." She held up her notes. "I wrote it down, but …"

"Good work." Mac pushed through the doors, and the cold air made her eyes water. She blinked and pulled on her gloves. "Let's get moving. We've got a lot to do today."

"Great. Where to next?" Zoe grinned as they hurried to the car. "Did you get the file you wanted?"

"It wasn't there." Mac slid into the passenger seat and cast a look at Zoe. "We'll talk later."

"Okay." Zoe did a slow nod and started the car.

Mac relaxed. Maybe her high school friend wasn't so bad after all. They navigated the few blocks to Leonard's auto repair shop in silence. Through an open garage door, Mac spied the rear end of her sedan.

Leonard ambled out, wiping his hands on a rag black with grease. He seemed impervious to the cold as he waited for Mac to get close enough to hear over the noise of air guns and whine of power tools.

"What do you think? Can you patch my tire?" Mac asked.

Leonard shook his head. "Too big a cut. You'll need a new tire, but I don't have any in stock. It'll take a couple days."

Her spirits sunk. There was something about not having

her car that made her feel vulnerable. She hated having to rely on someone else for a ride.

"Call me as soon as it's ready."

"I will."

She turned to go.

"Hang on." Leonard called her back. "I almost forgot. Part of the knife blade broke off. It was inside the tire. Thought you might want it—you being a private investigator."

"You thought right." New evidence always improved her outlook on life.

"I cleaned it off." He handed her a plastic bag. "Hope that was okay."

"Thanks, Leonard." Mac held the baggie up, and the weak winter light reflected off the knife tip inside. "You did just fine."

She retrieved her purse as she slid into the passenger's seat and stuffed the evidence bag inside. "You'll never guess what Leonard found. Part of the knife broke off in my tire."

"Cool." Zoe held out Mac's phone. "You left it in the car. You've got a message. It looks weird."

"What do you mean?"

"It showed on your screen, and I couldn't help seeing it." She gave a short laugh touched with embarrassment. "Sorry."

"I know you're looking for the treasure." Mac read the text aloud. "I can help." Instantly on guard, she scanned the area for the dark van. It wasn't in sight. She stepped out of the car and punched a number on her phone.

"Mackenzie Love and Samantha Majors, Private Investigators. How can I help you?"

"Miss P, is Sam there today?"

"She is, and she's rather irritated about being put on desk duty. Are you sure you want to talk to her? I could relay your message."

"No." Mac sighed. "I might as well get it over with."

"Very well."

"Yes?" Icicles dripped from Sam's voice.

"You can be mad if you want, but you and your sweet baby are too important to me. You might as well get over it." Mac listened and prayed. "Sam?"

"Mackenzie Love, I never could stay mad at you. It's so frustrating. What do you need?"

Thank you, Jesus.

"I need you to do a reverse check on a phone number." Mac read the text to Sam and the number. "Anything you can find. Plus, anything you can dig up on Brandon Fischer, Hank Young, and Owen Baker. I'll come into the office after lunch and tell you all about it."

"You'd better. I hate feeling like I'm too fragile to be a part of things around here."

Mac heard the tears in her friend's voice. "You and I are partners. I'm gathering evidence for you to analyze. When I'm done, we can sit down and figure out what's going on —together."

"I'm on it." Sam blew her nose. "See you later."

"Have you seen any sign of a dark van?" Mac closed the passenger side door and buckled up.

"No, no vans at all, dark or light." Zoe signaled and pulled onto the street. "Where to next?"

"The crime scene, Rennick Park."

"What do you make of your text?"

"I'm not sure." Mac read it again. "It's got to be referring to the contents of the time capsule. Although why call it treasure?"

"Maybe somebody else is looking for it too?"

"It seems that way. Or ..." A crazy thought skittered through her mind.

"Or what?" Zoe cut her eyes to Mac.

"Not yet. I need to think about it." She stared out the window. "When we get there, I'd like you to search around the capsule to see if you notice anything I didn't. Take pictures. I'm going to go over the day in my mind to see if I missed anything."

At the park, Mac climbed out of the car and walked with Zoe to the capsule. How long was it before the police showed up after she called 911? Fifteen minutes? Jake got there ten minutes later. He received the call about the murder less than an hour after he arrived. It wasn't much time to do what she was imagining. But, how much time did a man need to hide a coin?

CHAPTER 18

J ake tensed the moment he and Vic entered the Chief's office. Something was very wrong. Instead of sitting behind his desk, Chief Baker stood waiting for them, and as soon as Jake and Vic were inside, he closed and locked his door.

"Sit." The Chief paced around the small room, running his hand over his bald head. "Tell me what you found out from Fischer and Hank Young."

"Both men said the investment group only stayed together for a short while and they have a couple of properties, but that's it." Jake consulted his notes. "Brandon thought it was feasible that what he called a high stakes investor might try to pull off the theft."

The Chief stopped and stared at him. "Did he mention any names?"

"When I asked if he knew any, he said no, but I could see he wasn't telling the truth."

Chief Baker plopped into his chair. "Go on."

"But it turns out there may be another motive we didn't know about." Jake shared a look with Vic. "Mackenzie discovered the half-dollar on the list may be worth as much as two hundred *thousand* dollars."

The Chief turned pale.

"Sir, are you all right?" Vic rose.

Chief Baker motioned for the detective to sit once more. He cleared his throat. "I can't find my brother."

It took a minute for the pieces to fall into place in Jake's mind. "You're afraid he may be involved in this."

Baker nodded. "He's let himself be taken in by the wrong people before."

His boss aged before his eyes. The strong face sagged, and the alert gray eyes grew dim. Jake searched for something positive to say, but nothing came to him.

"He wouldn't kill anyone, but I could see him getting mixed up with whoever's in charge, especially with so much money involved." The grieving man put his head in his hands. "He's got lots of bills right now, and with Ivy in the hospital, he's about had it."

"Have you talked to your sister-in-law?"

"What do you think?" He gave Jake a piercing look. "If she knows anything, she's not saying, but I think she's as much in the dark as I am."

"Is he going to work?"

The older man shook his head. "He's been working for a construction company. His manager hasn't seen him for a week. If they weren't friends of the family, he'd be sacked by now."

"What happens when you call him? Is his phone going to voice mail?"

"It's off."

They couldn't track it. Jake stood, and Vic followed. "We'll find him, Chief. I'm sure there'll be—"

"Don't." The Chief held up his hands. "No platitudes. Just find him. And keep this to yourselves."

"What kind of car does he drive?" Vic pulled out his phone.

"A late model Honda van. Dark blue."

Like the one Mac saw outside her house. Suspicion knotted in Jake's stomach. He didn't believe in coincidences.

In the hallway, Vic stopped him. "How are we going to do this without help?"

"We're not."

"You heard him. Keep this to ourselves."

"We can still put out a BOLO on the van without saying what it's for."

"I don't know." Vic scratched his chin. "I don't think the old man will like it."

"Listen." Jake squared off with Vic. "We've got a theft and a murder to solve. I care about the Chief, but if his brother is involved, we need to find him. Fast. Before anyone else gets killed." Like Mackenzie. He strode back to his office and picked up the phone.

Vic trailed after him. "I don't get it. Why would anyone else be in danger if they already have the contents of the capsule?"

"The Chief believes his brother is working with someone. What if the other person decides he wants everything for himself?" Jake raised his eyebrows at his colleague. "He's killed once, what's stopping him from getting rid of the Chief's brother?" He raised a hand to stop Vic's reply and spoke into the phone. "I need a BOLO out on a navy blue 2021 Honda Odyssey."

"I'll check his cellphone records." Vic turned to go, his face grim.

"Hey," Jake said. "I'm glad we're working this together."

"Me too. Let me know if you hear anything."

"I will." Jake glanced at his watch. Time for a call to his sister before lunch.

When she answered, he listened for sounds of the television and Killer, her golden doodle, in the background, but heard neither. "Where are you?"

"Where are *you?*"

He cringed. Not the way to start the conversation with a hormonal woman—or any woman for that matter. "Sorry, sis. I meant to say, how are you?"

"Sure, you did." She snorted. "I'm fine. I'm at work if you haven't figured it out by now. Miss P is taking very good care of me, and the only thing I'm straining is my brain."

"Glad to hear it. What are you working on?"

"Mac has me doing research for our case."

"What kind of research?" His detective nose smelled something fishy.

"Oh, this and that."

"Samantha, you're hiding something. What is it?"

"I'd rather Mac tells you herself."

He didn't like the sound of that. "Did something happen to her?"

"Not exactly."

"What do you mean not exactly?" He fought to keep his voice even and lost.

"She got a weird text, okay? Now will you please let her tell you about it herself?"

"Yes." His jaw muscles released. "Is there anything you need?"

"No. Alan is coming by later with lunch for us. Thanks for calling, bro. I love you."

"Ditto." He pushed End and drummed his fingers on his desk. Weird text, huh? He pressed one on his phone.

Mac answered after one ring. "Hi, Jake. I'm about finished here. Are we still on for lunch? I asked Zoe to drop me off at the station if that's okay."

"Looking forward to it. We can share about the weird stuff that's happened today."

Silence.

"I'll be there in about half an hour."

He shouldn't have said that, but he couldn't help it. What was in the text, and why hadn't Mac shared it with him?

His phone rang again. "Sanders."

"Mr. Amory is on the line. He says he's remembered something else from the morning of the murder and wants to talk to you."

"Put him through." He let a trickle of hope run through him.

"Detective Sanders? Have you found the bicyclist yet?"

"No, sir."

"Too bad. Well, I've remembered something else that might help. It's not much. He—or she—was wearing red tennis shoes."

"Thanks, Mr. Amory. We appreciate your help."

"Of course. If there's anything I can do, just let me know."

After ending the call, Jake texted the information to Vic. If the suspect kept the shoes, it could be a big help, but most likely he'd trashed them. Right now, he needed to focus on another piece of information—the text to Mackenzie.

"JAKE MUST HAVE TALKED to his sister." Mac slipped her phone into her shoulder bag.

"What makes you say that?" Zoe looked up from where she crouched amongst the bushes next to the time capsule.

"He knows about my text, and he's upset."

"Got it." Her high school friend got to her feet and brushed her hands on her jeans. "I didn't find anything."

"I'm not surprised, but it's always good to have an extra pair of eyes on a scene." Mac swept her gaze over the parking lot once more. "You ready to go?"

A red sedan drove by on its way to the lower lot.

"That looks a lot like the one I saw at the museum earlier." Zoe took a step forward. "But I guess there's a lot of those around, and I don't know a thing about cars."

"Let's drive down and get the license plate before we leave."

But before they could, the car passed again on the way out. By the time they left the lot, the red sedan had disappeared.

"I guess it was just somebody cruising around. Probably a teenager in his mom's car."

"Yeah." Unease rippled up Mac's spine. Had he changed vehicles? "You need to get to work, and I need to get to the precinct."

On the short drive to the station house, Mac searched every cross street for a glimpse of red. The closer they got with no sign of the sedan, the more she relaxed. Maybe Zoe was right. Maybe it was just a teenager tooling around in his mother's car.

"Text me when you're finished at the restaurant, and I'll let you know where to pick me up. I may have Jake take me back to the office after lunch." She hopped out of the car and waved goodbye to Zoe.

Jake met her in the foyer. "Hi." He gave her a brief hug. "Old Dutch okay?"

"Are we walking?" She pulled her coat tighter around her. The restaurant wasn't far away, but she was freezing.

"No." He eyed her. "Too cold, and it looks like more snow."

The two and a half blocks distance wasn't enough for the SUV's heater to kick in, so it was a cold ride, but the advantage to driving was they got there faster, and for that, Mac was thankful. She made a beeline for their favorite spot, a table for two in the back along the wall.

After ordering, Jake folded his hands on the table and gave her a big smile. "Okay. Who's going to share her weird stuff first?"

"Or his." She mimicked his pose. "How did your meeting with the Chief go?" His blue eyes darkened at her challenge. Would he speak or maintain his silence, trying to force her to reveal her information first?

"The Chief's brother, Owen, is missing."

She hadn't expected that, and she knew it showed on her face. "You're kidding."

"I wish I was." He relaxed. "The Chief believes Owen is involved in the theft and murder somehow."

"Poor man. As if he doesn't have enough to worry about."

"One other thing." He reached for her hand. "Owen drives a dark blue Honda van."

"What?" She tried to pull her hand away, but Jake held it tight. Owen Baker, her stalker? Why?

"Take it easy. I put out a BOLO on it. We should be hearing something soon." He released her hand and sat back. "I can't believe he's our killer, but I do believe he's mixed up with one."

The waitress brought their food and drinks. After a few bites, Mac stopped and stared at her plate.

"I'm trying to make sense of all this. Why would Owen be following me?"

"Let me help. Tell me about the text you got today."

"Sam told you, didn't she?" Mac lifted her eyes to his.

"I didn't give her much choice."

"I'll start with the file—the one containing the names of everyone who knows what was contained in the time capsule. Remember I went to the museum to retrieve it?"

He nodded.

"It's missing. There was a meeting at the museum last night, and I've asked Mrs. White to make a list of who was there. She's doing so reluctantly."

"What do you mean reluctantly?"

"She has a hard time believing anyone in our fair city would steal."

Jake snorted. "She needs to spend a day with me."

"That would only depress her." Mac sipped her iced tea. "Our next stop was Leonard's."

"Let me guess. He found the file in your car. It was there all the time."

"No. I wish." Mac rooted in her purse and pulled out the clear plastic bag. "But he did find a broken piece of the knife in my tire." She handed it to Jake.

"Are we getting to the text?"

"Yes." She threw him a quick smile. "The message was on my phone as I got back in Zoe's car at Leonard's. Here. You can read it for yourself."

"I know you're looking for the treasure. I can help." He handed her phone back. "That's it?"

She nodded. "What do you think?"

"Send it to me." He took a bite of his burger and slowly chewed.

Mac waited until he swallowed. "Well?"

"It sounds like either someone else is looking for the contents of the capsule—or ..."

"Or?" She leaned forward. Would Jake come to the same conclusion she had?

His eyes met hers in a look filled with common understanding. She shivered.

"Or the head guy wants to partner with you because the item he wants most from the time capsule wasn't in the bag Freddy gave him. He's hoping you'll find it for him."

CHAPTER 19

"The mule coin." Excitement danced through Mac. Jake got it. "It's the only thing that makes sense, and it's small enough Freddy could have hidden it before meeting Mr. Big."

"Mr. Big?" Jake raised an eyebrow at her.

"What else can I call him?"

"You're probably right, but the stamp would be easy to hide too. We're in the process of investigating that and the map."

"Of course." Mac's hunger returned, and she finished off her sandwich.

Jake eyed her. "But you're certain it's the coin."

She nodded as she sipped her tea.

"You may be right. I got the autopsy report back today. It seems the killer turned out all the victim's pockets and removed his shoes and socks."

"Like Mr. Big was searching for something." Satisfaction bubbled through Mac. Watch out, Mr. Big, she was on the trail.

"I know a little about your Mr. Big. Remember?" Jake wiped

his mouth. "We have a witness who saw a man on a bicycle leaving the scene at about the time of the murder. He couldn't tell us much, but he said the man had on a ski mask, black jacket, and skinny ski pants with a red stripe. Oh, and red tennis shoes."

Mac jotted the description down in her notebook. "What type of bike was it?"

"A mountain bike. Black. We think."

"You don't know?"

"The guy said it had fat tires. Not a racing bike." Jake pointed to her list. "And saddlebags."

"Anything else?"

"He had a ponytail hanging out the back of his ski mask. Dishwater blond."

Mac nodded and scribbled on her pad.

"You know what dishwater blond is?"

"Of course." She looked at him. "Doesn't everybody?"

"You follow up on the coin, and I'll keep at the others. Deal?" He sighed. "And send me any more texts or other communications you get. That's an order."

She gave him The Look.

"Please."

"Drop me at the office, okay?" She couldn't wait to run all this by Sam and Miss P.

Jake paid their bill, and they walked around the building to where he parked on West Third Street.

At the car, Mac turned and pecked Jake on the cheek. "Thanks for lunch."

He leaned in and skimmed his lips along the sweep of her cheek until he got to her lips. Goosebumps clothed her skin, and her mind went blank. He released her and opened the car door.

She collapsed onto the passenger's seat. "You don't play fair, Jake Sanders."

"I know." He grinned at her. "But you know what they say about love and war."

"Yep." She put her hand on the door handle.

He snatched his arm out of the way as she yanked the door shut and grinned back at him. The tingle from his kiss lasted all the way to the office, and she hesitated before exiting the SUV.

"You free tonight?" He brought her hand to his mouth and pressed a soft kiss on her palm.

"Yes." She felt the heat of a blush on her cheeks. What was that all about? They'd been dating for months.

"Good. I'll pick you up at seven." He let go of her hand and got out to come around and open her door.

She narrowed her gaze. What was he up to? Jake was always considerate, respectful, and loving, but this behavior was new.

He pulled her in for another kiss before walking her to the door. "I'll see you later."

Mac shut the door and took off her gloves, still pondering what had just happened. Not that she didn't like Jake's kisses, she loved them, but it was like a switch had been thrown. What did she say or do at lunch to make him behave in such a way? Nothing. At least she couldn't think of anything.

"Mackenzie, are you all right?" Miss P bustled across the room to help her with her coat.

"I'm fine." She moved to the large table in the center of the room where they gathered to share information and go over cases. "We need to put our heads together."

"It's about time." Sam carried her laptop to her usual spot. "I feel like the ugly stepsister."

"I'll get us some refreshments." Miss P gave Mac a look over Sam's head before leaving for the kitchen.

"How was your morning with Zoe?" Sam pounded on her keyboard, and her screen sprang to life.

"Not too bad. But it's only the first day, and it's not over yet."

"I'm sure you'll do fine. You guys were friends in high school. Way before you met me."

Mac pushed her chair back and went over to her friend. "Zoe may be an old friend, but you're my best friend. No one could or ever will take your place in my heart, Sam." She gave her partner a hug.

Sam stood and buried her face in Mac's shoulder. "Why am I so emotional these days?"

"Your hormones are going wacky. What did the doctor say?"

"He gave me vitamins." She regained her seat and swiped at her eyes.

"I'm sure your moods will stabilize soon, my dear." Miss P sat glasses of iced tea and a plate of cookies on the table. She pushed a box of tissues within Sam's reach. "And I believe concentrating on work will help immensely."

"I think so too." Mac looked at her notes. "Were you able to get a license number from the photos I sent you?"

"No. Your camera lens fogged up in the cold." Sam swiveled her computer to show her the pictures.

"I was afraid of that." She gnawed on a cuticle. "I may know who it is anyway. Jake found out Owen Baker drives a dark blue Honda Odyssey."

"The Chief's brother? Why would he be following you?"

"Remember the phone number I asked you to track?"

Sam nodded.

"I got a text from the number. Here." Mac passed her phone

to Sam and Miss P. "The short story is Jake and I think Freddy hid something from the time capsule before meeting with Mr. Big, and—"

"Mr. Big?"

"The guy in charge." Mac waved a hand in the air. "And Mr. Big discovered what happened after he had already killed Freddy. Now he's got Owen following me, hoping I'll lead him to the item he wants."

"Does Jake know anything about this Mr. Big?"

"Maybe. A witness saw a man on a bicycle leaving the scene of the murder. He gave Jake a vague description. Here are my notes." Mac pushed her pad across the table to Sam.

"Red shoes and long dark blond hair aren't much to go on."

"I know, but it's better than nothing."

A knock sounded at the door.

"I'll get it." Miss P stood and crossed the room. "May I help you?"

"It's me, Zoe Dixon, Miss Freebody." She threw her arms around the older lady.

Miss P gently extricated herself from the woman's embrace. "Of course, my dear. Come in."

"I texted but didn't get an answer, so I called Jake. He told me you were here." The blonde woman took off her coat, revealing her curvaceous figure.

Mac closed her eyes and fought back the spike of jealousy that reared its ugly head.

"Does the Chief truly believe Owen could be involved with the theft and Freddy's murder?" Compassion and pity played over Miss P's face.

"He's the one who suggested it to Jake."

"I'm sorry. You lost me." Zoe scrunched up her face. "Who's Freddy? And Owen?"

"Freddy ... actually, in the interest of time, I'll have Miss P make a copy of the file so you can read it tonight."

"Speaking of files, did you get the one from the museum?" Sam stopped typing to look at Mac.

"It wasn't there. Somebody either took it, or it's been misplaced."

"What do you think?"

"I think it was stolen. The Downtown Merchants Group met there last night. I'm getting a list of names."

A text chimed on Mac's phone. Things were looking up. "I guess I was wrong." She surged to her feet and motioned to Zoe. "Mrs. White has found the file. We're going back to the museum. We'll see you guys later."

As they stepped outside, snowflakes whispered through the air once more. Mac flipped her hood up and pulled on her gloves. "How's your car in this weather?"

"It's all-wheel drive. We shouldn't have any trouble." Zoe looked at her feet clad in tennis shoes. "I wish I'd worn my boots."

"This shouldn't take long. You'll be okay."

For the second time that day, they pulled into the museum parking lot, and Mac left Zoe by the glass front door while she went in search of Mrs. White. The historian bustled across the room with a manilla envelope in her hand.

"One of the young women found it in the copy room. I have no idea how it got there."

The historian's eyes gleamed with goodwill once more. "But I was glad to see it hadn't been taken like you thought."

Mac tucked the package under her arm and gave the woman a brief hug. "Thanks for letting me know so soon." No, it hadn't been taken, but it had been moved. To the copy room. "Just out of curiosity, who has access to your copier?"

"I suppose anyone." She shrugged. "We allow patrons to copy in there too."

"Do they have to sign a register or anything?"

"No."

"Is there any way to tell what's been copied?"

"Not really." Mrs. White barked a laugh. "Mackenzie, you do ask a lot of questions. I suppose it goes with your profession. I have the list of people who were here last evening. Do you want it?"

"Yes, thank you." She smiled at her friend. "I'm sorry for bothering you."

"No bother. It's only ... I could never do what you do. The constant suspicion would wear me out." The historian walked with her to the door.

She'd never thought of her job that way. She supposed that was how it must seem to others. To her, each case was a puzzle to be solved by gathering information until she had enough to see the complete picture.

"Wait a minute." Zoe held her arm out and blocked Mac from leaving. "Is that the van you saw this morning?"

A pulse of adrenaline spurted through her, making her heart race. She stepped behind Zoe and peered over her shoulder. "Where?"

"Parked across the street. It passed twice and then it stopped within sight of both doors of the museum."

"It looks like the same one." Mac pulled her temporary partner away from the glass doors. "Let me think."

"Is there a problem?" Mrs. White asked.

She eyed her friend. "Could I borrow your coat and hat for a moment?"

"I ... certainly."

The historian left and returned with a long gray woolen

coat and hat to match. Mackenzie slipped into the coat and stuffed her long hair up under the hat.

"May I ask what this is all about?"

"I'm being followed by a blue van, and I think it's parked over there." She pointed across the parking lot. "I'm hoping your coat will disguise me enough to get close and see who it is."

"Oh my." Wrinkles of worry furrowed her brow. "Please be careful."

Mac pulled the hat down over her face and shoved her hands into the pockets of Mrs. White's coat.

She concentrated on appearing older and shorter. But, the smaller steps and slower pace were agonizing, and the desire to rush the van pushed at her resolve with every stride. Finally, the curb came into view of her down-turned eyes. She veered left and started her slow progress down the sidewalk.

After about ten feet, she stepped off the curb, acted as if she slipped, caught herself, and crossed the street. The van hadn't moved. This was the most critical part. She would be facing the driver as she continued her snaillike movement up the sidewalk on the other side of the street.

Her heartbeat ramped up the closer she came to her prey. As she passed the van, she hazarded a quick glance at the passenger side window. The tint prevented her from seeing inside. At the second parked car beyond the van, she ducked and moved behind it to the side of the vehicles facing the street. Her target lay less than one hundred feet from her. Sweat trickled down her spine, and she considered removing the coat. But there was no place to lay the garment that wasn't snow covered.

She needed to move, or she'd miss her chance. She sprinted for the driver's door of the van and yanked it open. The cold metal of the handle barely registered on her skin.

"Why are you following me?" The words escaped her mouth before her brain processed the scene in front of her. When it did, the next thing out of her mouth was a scream.

CHAPTER 20

Mac slammed the car door and fumbled in her pockets for her phone before it dawned on her. This wasn't her coat. She whirled around to face the museum just as the *whoop whoop* of a police car sounded behind her. How had they arrived so soon? She turned to greet them.

"Stop. Police."

"Thank God. I don't know how—" Mac took a step toward the police officer.

"Stay right there, ma'am." He put his hand on his gun.

"I'm the one who called it in." She raised her hands, palms out. "Well, not me, but Zoe, I imagine. It's gruesome." She lowered her hands.

"Is this your vehicle?" He unsnapped the guard on his holster "Put your hands on the vehicle."

"It's not my van." She complied. The cold of the metal traveled through her hands and up her arms into her whole body. "I just told you. I called nine-one-one. What's the problem?"

"Mac, are you all right?" Zoe ran across the street.

"Stay there, miss." The officer held out his left hand and keyed his mic on his shoulder. "I need back-up at my location, ASAP."

"May I ask why you stopped?" Mac kept her hands on the van and used her most respectful voice.

"There's a BOLO out on your vehicle."

"It's not my ..." She sighed. "You're going to need a lot more than backup." Mac looked at him over her shoulder. "I'm Mackenzie Love, and this is my partner, Zoe. We're private investigators, and there's a dead man sitting in the driver's seat of this van."

The officer muttered something under his breath and keyed his mic once more. "I have a ten-fifty-four at my location. Repeat, a ten-fifty-four."

"May I turn around now?"

"Yes, but keep your hands where I can see them, and I need to see some ID."

"This isn't my coat. It's a long story." Mac nodded toward the museum. "My wallet's in there."

"And I don't have an ID. I'm only a temp." Zoe shrugged.

He furrowed his brow as if trying to work through how to handle the situation. "We'll wait in my car, but I'll have to cuff the two of you."

"That's so stupid." Zoe put her hands on her hips.

"Just do it." Mac held out her hands. "At least it's warm in there." And she would be farther away from the horror inside the van.

After they were settled in the back seat of the patrol car, she motioned for Zoe to keep quiet. They sat in silence for what seemed like hours but was only minutes.

"You're sure the guy was dead?" The officer glanced at her in the rearview mirror.

"I'm certain." Mac shuddered. "His throat had been cut."

She waited for his curiosity to get the better of him. It wouldn't be long. The question was, had he ever seen a dead body before?

"I'd better check." A chill breeze swept through the car as the police officer left and walked toward the van.

He hitched his gun belt up on his waist. When he drew level with the driver's window, he leaned closer and peered in, but Mac knew the windows were too dark to see through. He opened the door, took a step back, slammed the door, and hurried around the front of the van. For a few moments, he disappeared.

He managed a rocky swagger back to his police car. "Definitely a homicide."

Sirens converged on them from all sides, and the police officer got out to consult with a group of men. A familiar figure broke away from the huddle, and Mac groaned.

The back door opened on her side. Again, cold air rushed into the car, and Jake squatted outside beside her. "I always knew you'd end up in handcuffs one day." His blue eyes twinkled above the smirk spread across his face.

She'd expected his reaction, and any other time she'd have bantered back with him, but this time was different. "Not now, Jake." She worked to hold back her tears. The sight of the man with his throat slit had shocked her.

"I'm sorry, Mac." Jake's manner changed in an instant to one of compassion and caring. "No one should have to see that." He leaned in and unlocked the handcuffs.

"Me too." Zoe stuck out her hands.

He keyed hers open and backed out of the car. "Did you recognize the victim?"

Mac rubbed her wrists and shook her head. "All I saw was a hideous red gash with the head at a strange angle." She looked at Jake. "Should I have?"

"Seems the Chief was right." He ran a hand through his hair. "It's Owen."

Her legs gave for a moment, and she reached for Jake. "We have to find who did this."

"No, the police will find this guy." He faced her. "You need to stay out of his way."

"I have a case to finish." Her eyes slammed into his. "And I never back out on a case."

"Do I have to put you back in handcuffs?"

"Uh, guys." Zoe stepped closer. "Take it down a notch, okay?"

"Come on." Mac strode away as best she could in boots through an inch of new snow. "We have work to do." She glanced back to see Jake staring after her, his face shadowed with concern. Why did he have to be so controlling? Didn't he realize she took her job as seriously as he did his?

"I knew I should have worn boots. My feet are soaking wet." Zoe caught up to her as they crossed the museum parking lot. "What's next?"

"I'll give Mrs. White her coat and get my things. Afterward, it's back to the office for another groupthink. You can drop me off and go home if you need to."

"Do you mind?" Zoe's mouth turned up in a brief grin. "I met this guy at lunch, and he asked me out on a date tonight."

"Just be sure not to talk about anything we did today."

Mrs. White waited for them inside the door. "What happened over there? Did you talk to the man? I was so frightened."

"I'm afraid he's dead." Mac handed the historian her coat. "I'm sorry. I can't say anymore. Thank you for the use of your coat."

"Oh dear." She held it away from her like it was contaminated.

"It's fine. I didn't get close to him. I promise." Mac pulled on her jacket and gloves. She looked at Zoe. "Do you have my files?"

"Yes." She held up the manilla envelope.

"We need to go, Mrs. White. Thank you for all your help."

As they left the parking lot, Mac caught sight of the distressed woman standing at the door staring at the van. She should have stayed with Mrs. White a little longer. Assured her it had nothing to do with the museum or her, and that the police had things in hand. But how could she comfort someone else when she needed comforting herself?

Visions of Owen Baker with his throat cut looped through her mind over and over. She pressed her fingers to her forehead. *Lord, make it stop.*

"Were you and the dead guy friends?" Zoe signaled for a turn at the corner.

"I was friends with his daughter, Ivy."

"Ivy Baker? From school?" She swiveled her head in Mac's direction for an instant. "The guy in the van was her dad?"

Mac nodded. She'd forgotten Zoe and Ivy were friends too.

"Oh man. Poor Ivy. This is going to be really hard on her."

Tears filled Mac's eyes. Zoe had no idea what had happened to her friend. Ivy already battled with depression. She couldn't bear to think what this would do to her. She might not survive it. They pulled into the driveway at the office, and Mac jumped out of the car.

"I'll see you in the morning. Same time. Have fun tonight." She raced off before Zoe could respond.

Inside the familiar warm room, she dropped her purse and files and hurried to a chair in the reception area where she hugged her knees to her chest. Waves of sorrow and fatigue washed through her, and silent tears streamed down her face, drenching the front of her coat.

Miss P appeared at her side with a cup of something hot. "Drink this, my dear."

"What is it?"

"It's lemon balm tea with sugar. It will calm you."

Mac wrapped her hands around the cup and inhaled the soothing aroma.

"Take a sip." Miss P ran a gentle hand over the top of Mac's head. "We heard what happened on the police band radio."

"It must have been awful finding Mr. Baker that way." Sam came up next to her.

"I didn't realize it was him." Mac unfurled her legs. "How could I not recognize Ivy's dad?"

"You were in shock."

"I guess." She took a deep breath. "I keep thinking about Ivy and what this will do to her."

"Maybe they'll wait to tell her until she's able to deal with it." Sam placed a hand on her stomach.

"I hope so."

"We'll pray for her." Miss P took the cup from Mac. "However, now I believe it's time we got to work, don't you think?"

Mac stood and squared her shoulders. "I'll get my things." Thank God for Miss P and her keen sense of discernment. Work was just what she needed.

Seated once more at their multipurpose table, she jotted some notes about what happened. Her tension built as she wrote, and her hand began to shake.

"Let me get you another cup of tea." Miss P paused at the kitchen door. "Will Zoe be joining us this evening?"

"No. I gave her the night off. She's got a date."

"Who with?" Sam threw her a concerned look. "How did she meet him?"

"At the restaurant this afternoon." Mac waved a hand in the air. "What does it matter?"

"What restaurant?"

Mac stopped writing and scowled at her partner. "She worked a shift at the Skillet while Jake and I had lunch. She met him there. Is that okay with you?"

"No." Sam flashed back at her. "We should know who he is. What if she's walking into a trap?"

"Who would want to hurt Zoe?"

"The man in charge. Mr. Big. By now he knows she's working with us."

Mac grabbed her phone and prayed as she dialed Zoe's number.

After four rings, it went to voicemail.

CHAPTER 21

Why hadn't Mac questioned Zoe about her date when she had the chance? She'd been so wrapped up in her own problems, she hadn't even thought about her partner being in any danger. Now, her friend from high school could be lying somewhere hurt or dying, and she had no idea where.

She pressed redial.

"Hi, Mac. What's up?"

"Hi, Zoe." Relief left Mac weak. She pressed Speaker. "Sam and I were talking, and we decided while we're working on this case it would be best if we all kept tabs on each other."

"What does that mean?"

Best get to the point. "Who are you going out with this evening?"

"I get it. You're worried about my safety." Zoe laughed. "Not necessary. He's a perfect gentleman. He just got back into town. Like me."

Mac waited for Zoe's answer, but she already knew his name. A name that kept popping up, and one that left her feeling uneasy.

"David Rush, the famous painter."

"Where are you going?"

"We're meeting at Cowan's for dinner. What are *you* doing this evening?" Zoe's clipped words snapped from the speaker.

Mac almost said "none of your business" but caught herself. "Jake and I are going for dinner. I'm not sure where. Would you like me to text you when we decide?"

"Not necessary. See you tomorrow." The hang-up buzz reverberated in the room.

"Well, that went well, didn't it?" Sam widened her eyes at Mac.

"I've got a funny feeling about Rush." Mac stared at her phone. "I can't put my finger on it, but I'd like to know more about him. I mean, why if he's such a successful painter living in New York, would he want to come back to Washington, Missouri?"

"You could try asking Zoe tomorrow, but I'm not sure she'll be too cooperative." Sam chuckled. "I think it would be better if Miss P and I do some research."

"Unfortunately, none of this gets us any closer to discovering where the memorabilia from the time capsule is at this moment." Miss P pushed her chair away from the table. "And that's what we have been hired to do, ladies." She stopped. "But the name David Rush does remind me of what I was trying to remember about the Koenig boys. After their parents died, they lived with David and his aunt for a time until Freddy found a job and was able to support he and his brother, Tim."

"So, David would have known Freddy." Mac's gaze unfocused as she pondered the significance of this information.

"He was closer to Tim's age, but yes, he certainly would have been acquainted with Freddy as well. But again, while this may be interesting to Detective Sanders, it doesn't help us find what was stolen from the time capsule. Unless David Rush is involved of course."

"True. Let's start by listing motives for breaking into the capsule in the first place." Mac turned to a fresh piece of paper. "The mule coin has to be at the top."

"The question becomes who knew the coin was in there." Miss P peered at Mac over her glasses. "Wasn't that supposed to be in the file you got from Mrs. White?"

"Yes." Mac dug the manila folder from the stack next to her. "Would you make copies of this?"

"What other possible motives could there be?"

"It could be the plans for the city or the parks like Jake originally thought. Which would put a developer back in the picture."

Sam nodded.

"The police also found out there was a rare Bible, an antique map, and a valuable stamp with the remembrances in the capsule. If the thief didn't know how valuable the half dollar was, it could have been one of those he was after."

"I guess it hinges on who knew what was in there and how valuable it was."

"Exactly." Mac doodled question marks across the top of her page. "If we can do that, we'll be able to find what was taken from the time capsule."

"I'm afraid this won't be an easy task." Miss P handed copies to Mac and Sam. "It's a very long list and includes relatives of most of the people we've talked about."

"Which means any of them could have known the contents of the capsule." Sam sighed.

"Not quite." Mac ran her eyes down the list of names. "The Bible, the map, and the stamp were added at the last minute. Only a few people could have known about them. Besides, I have another idea about the theft that could help us find what we're looking for."

"Well, I vote we leave it until tomorrow." Sam pushed away from the table. "I'm too tired and too hungry to think about anything else tonight."

Mac opened her mouth to protest but stopped herself. A ripple of sadness passed through her as she realized things were changing. Her friend and partner was having a baby—a blessing for sure, but life would never be the same again. No more late-night sessions discussing cases. No more taking off at a moment's notice. No more partnership?

Sam pulled on her coat and gloves.

Mac popped up and threw her arms around her friend.

"Hey. It's not like I'm leaving forever." Sam studied her face. "Everything's going to be okay. I'll see you tomorrow."

Mac smiled at her. How did Sam always seem to know what to say? It was like she could read Mac's mind.

Sam drove a lot slower these days. In fact, she did a lot of things differently. The thought that she carried another life inside her left her awestruck.

As she left the office, her body tightened in response to an inner warning system that had her peering into the darkness. The moon and stars hid behind clouds, and the night was filled with shadows. A chill wind hit her the moment she stepped off the porch, and she wished she'd had Alan bring her to work so he'd be picking her up.

Inside her SUV, she turned the heater up to full blast and tuned into the local Christian music station. The closer she got to home, the more relaxed she became.

"Silly," she said to herself. "I'm not afraid of a few shadows. I'm a trained private investigator."

At last, she was on familiar territory. She sped up and turned off her radio. The windows of her house glowed in the darkness. Her headlights arced into her driveway, sweeping over the hedge along the property line.

A man dressed in black ran in front of her. Sam hit the brakes. He slapped the windshield, pushed through the hedge, and disappeared. Her pulse pounded in her throat, and for a moment she sat, engine running and foot on the brake.

Her breathing slowed, and she put the car in drive. That's when she noticed it. The man had thrust a note onto her windshield. Was he waiting for her to get out of the car so he could grab her?

She shifted into Park, peered into the darkness, and dialed Alan's number with shaky fingers.

"Where are you? I thought you'd be home by now." Furious barking sounded in the background. "Hush, Killer."

"I'm in the driveway. A man—"

Alan and Killer burst out the front door and raced to her car. He flung open her door.

"Are you hurt?" He yanked on her arm.

"Let me unbuckle." She pulled away and released her seat belt. "I'm fine. I didn't want to get out in case he was still around."

"Good thinking."

Killer, their goldendoodle, continued to bark and stood on his back legs, extending his front paws toward them.

"It's okay, pooch." Sam scratched his head and took his proffered paw. "Everything's fine."

"Which way did he go?" Alan swiveled around.

"Through the hedge. But—" Sam put a hand on his arm.

"I'm sure he's gone. I'm more interested in the note he left behind."

Alan reached for it.

"Don't. I need to get a baggie. There may be prints."

"In this weather? He'd have on gloves."

"Not when he wrote it."

"Beauty and brains." Alan gave his wife a quick kiss. "I'll wait here."

Sam hurried inside and returned a moment later with a large zipper baggie and gloves. She resisted the urge to try to read the note and placed it in the bag. "I'm going in. Okay?"

"I'll pull your car up and join you in a sec," Alan said.

In the kitchen, Sam extracted the note and laid it on a clean paper towel. She squinted at the grimy scrap of paper, its black letters smudged from the wet glass of the windshield. Alan came up behind her.

"What does it say?"

"Time is of the essence. You must HURRY." Something tugged at her memory. She retrieved her phone and took a photo of it to send to Mac.

"Sam, answer me," Alan said. "What does it mean? Does it have anything to do with your latest case? Are you in danger?"

She turned to face him, pulling his arms around her. "I'm not in any danger. It does have to do with our case, but it's more of a clue to help us than a threat."

"How so?" He tightened his hold on her.

"I'm not sure, but I have an idea."

CHAPTER 22

Mac stroked Duchess's sleek gray fur and watched as the kittens stalked and pounced on each other over and over. She sighed with contentment. There was nothing like a group of clumsy little balls of fur romping around to take a girl's mind off her work.

"Are you sure eating here is okay?" Jake stuck his head around the kitchen doorway. "All I've got is salad and French bread."

"It's purrfect."

Jake groaned. "You know, you're welcome to one of those bundles of fur anytime."

"They're not ready to leave their mom yet, are they?"

"No, they're only about six weeks old. But when they are, you can have one. Or all four if you want."

"Hah. Hah. I might take one, but no way are you getting me to take all of them." Her thoughts were interrupted by a ping from her phone. "It's Sam." Mac lifted Duchess off her lap and went into the kitchen.

"What's the matter?" Jake dropped his knife and looked over Mac's shoulder at her phone.

"She got a note from some man." Fear for her friend squeezed Mac's heart like a steel band. "I'm going to call her." When Sam answered, Mac punched Speaker. "I'm with your brother. What happened?"

"It's not a big deal." Sam's brusque reply echoed in the room. "Alan and I took care of it."

"We were worried about you."

"You don't need to be. I can take care of myself."

Mac drew in a breath. Calling her was a bad idea. "Okay. Sorry. I didn't mean to imply you couldn't."

Silence ticked by.

"I'm sorry, Mac. I'm tired, and it scared me at first. The guy jumped out from nowhere."

"What do you think the note means?" Tension bled away from Mac. Another fight averted.

"I think it's a clue. Maybe to where we should be looking? But I'm too tired to figure it out tonight."

"Yeah. We'll talk about it in the morning. I just wanted to hear your voice. To know you were okay. See you tomorrow."

"Love you."

"Ditto." Mac pushed End.

Jake gathered her into his arms and stroked her hair. "Sam's not herself right now."

"Isn't that the truth." Mac wrapped her arms around his waist. "I miss her."

"I know. Me too."

Duchess strode into the room with four mewing kittens close behind. Her emerald gaze focused on Jake as she assumed a regal pose before her food dish.

"I think I'm being summoned." Jake released Mac with a

chuckle. "Can you slice the bread while I give her highness her food?"

A smile lifted the corners of Mac's mouth. She couldn't help it. When the kittens were around, their zest for life didn't leave any room for gloom. "I'll be glad to. I'm hungry."

Mac and Jake ate in the kitchen while Duchess finished her meal one dainty bite at a time, and the kittens slurped their wet food from bowls of their own. Sated, the little bundles of fur fell asleep on the rug in a heap.

"I'll help clean up, and you can take me home." Mac gathered the dishes off the table and walked to the sink.

She ached to stay, but she was getting too comfortable with letting Jake play such an important role in her life. He hadn't said anything about their future, and she needed to steel herself for a time when she may be on her own again.

"I can do that later." He slid his arms around her from behind and kissed the side of her neck.

Her pulse sped up.

"It's nice seeing you here in my kitchen." He kissed her earlobe. "I could get used to this."

Maybe she'd read him wrong. "I'm not really very domestic." She forced the words past the lump in her throat.

"We'll manage."

She turned to face him. What did he mean by that comment? "If you're asking me to live with you, the answer's no."

"I'd never ask you to do that." He held her away from him.

"What do you mean?"

He stroked her arm. "I mean it's time we get serious."

She drew in a quick breath as the implications of his words hit her. "Jake, are you asking me to marry you?" She placed a hand on his chest.

"No, no." His eyes widened.

She stepped back. "You want me to be your housekeeper or what?"

"Of course not." He closed the distance between them. "At least not right now. I mean, right now we'd be serious, and marriage would be later. I think it's time we get serious."

"You said that." She pushed him away. "Jake Sanders, you are the most frustrating man I know. Take me home. It's been a long day."

"That didn't come out the way I meant it." He ran a hand through his hair.

"We'll talk more tomorrow."

On one level, she understood what he was saying. But her heart yearned for something more permanent. And what would happen when Jake found out about her family history? Would he change his mind? Was she strong enough to take the chance?

"Jake, I love you so much."

"And I love you, Mackenzie."

In the car, her stomach churned. Jake wanted to get serious, which could mean a proposal in the future. That part filled her with joy, but there was the other part. The part no one knew about except her sisters and their husbands. Should she tell Jake now before they got too far in this serious relationship?

Her mind was so busy with this dilemma she almost didn't notice the red car parked in the same place as the blue van. When Jake pulled into her driveway, it took off.

"Did you see the red car that pulled away as we pulled in?"

"No. Why?"

"Zoe and I have noticed it around in the last couple of days."

"Are you sure it's the same car?"

"No, but it looks like it."

"You think it's someone else keeping an eye on you?"

"I don't know. Maybe I'm being paranoid." She stared down the street.

"Hey." Jake turned her face toward his. "I trust your instincts. I'll have a patrol car drive by periodically tonight. If they see a red sedan, they'll stop it and see who it is."

"Thanks. I'd appreciate it."

"Talk to you tomorrow." She hopped out of the SUV and ran up to her door before he could respond.

His car door slammed, and she heard him call her name. She waved and sprinted inside. So much had happened, and she needed time to process it all. Time to regroup. Time to pray. She slung her coat and purse on the sofa and walked down the hall to her bedroom.

Her antique floor lamp cast a soft light on the upholstered chair in the corner. Every time Mac sat there it was as if she were sitting on her mother's lap once more. She reached for her Bible and let it fall open on its own. The book of Psalms. One of her favorites. In the semidarkness, she began to read.

A RAY of sunlight poked through the blinds, stabbing Mackenzie in her left eye. She lifted her head from the back of the chair and ran her tongue over cracked lips. Every muscle protested as she reached for her phone.

Seven thirty. Time to get moving. She picked up her Bible from the floor where it fell. It lay open to Proverbs, chapter twenty-three. Her eye caught on verse twenty-three, and she read it aloud.

"Get the truth and never sell it; also get wisdom, discipline, and good judgment." She closed the book and placed it on the table. "I try, Lord, but it's not easy."

She heard the distinctive sound of her phone and raced to answer it.

"Miss Love? Your car is ready. Want me to bring it by?"

"Leonard, you made my day." Her spirits rose. "I'll be here."

After a few stretches, a shower, and breakfast, Mac was ready to face the day. Especially since she had her wheels back. She surveyed the street before backing out of her driveway. No red car was visible anywhere, and the tension released from her shoulders and neck. Maybe she was being paranoid.

Her phone chimed, and Sam's name popped up on the screen on her dashboard. She pressed a button. "Good morning, partner."

"Where are you?"

"Almost there." She braked for the stop sign at High Street and W Third Street. "About seven—" Motion in her rearview mirror captured her attention.

A red sedan raced at her from behind.

Mac clenched the steering wheel and prepared for impact.

The car screeched to a stop inches from her bumper and reversed, it's engine whining. She watched, frozen in place as it performed a high speed one-eighty and raced away.

"Mac, are you there? What's going on?"

CHAPTER 23

Mac closed her eyes and took a deep breath. He was gone. No harm done. "I'm okay. I'll tell you when I get there." She pressed the hang up button on her steering wheel and turned right on West Third.

At the office, Miss P met her at the door with a cup of hot tea.

"Is this more of your lemon balm tea?" Mac chuckled.

"Yes, I made it special for you." The older woman peered at her over the rim of her glasses.

"Thank you." Chastened, she dropped her purse on a chair and took an appreciative sip of the warm beverage.

"Are you going to tell us what happened to you this morning?" Sam stood in her doorway, arms folded across her chest.

"A red sedan's been showing up at the museum and the park the last couple of days. Last night, I saw it parked across from my house."

"A blue van and now a red sedan?"

"I know. Crazy." Mac sank into her chair. "This morning, I was at the stop sign at Third Street when the car barreled down on me out of nowhere. It was so fast, I didn't have time to react."

"I didn't hear a collision."

"He managed to stop two inches from my bumper." The remarkable incident replayed in her mind.

"Did you get a look at the driver?"

Mac shook her head. "He did a reverse one-eighty so fast I didn't get the chance. Besides, his windows were tinted."

"Why would he pull a stunt like that?" Sam slapped her hand on the table. "It makes no sense."

"I believe he wants to make sure he has your attention." Miss P tented what were once elegant fingers in front of her face. "But why he wishes for you to notice his automobile is beyond me."

"Maybe it's another clue." Sam opened her computer.

"I hate ambiguous clues." Mac opened her notepad to a clean page. "But let's see what we've got so far."

"Here's the note left on my windshield." Sam handed the baggie to Mac.

"Time is of the essence. You must HURRY." It seemed he wanted them to focus on the word hurry. But why?

"It occurs to me another word for hurry is rush," Miss P said. "Might that be what is intended here?"

"As in David Rush? Have either of you had time to do any research on him?"

"I have." Miss P pulled a folder over from a stack next to her. "And I found a few things worth noting." Her lips moved silently as she found what she wanted on the paper in front of her. "Before arriving back in Washington, there is a two-year gap in information available about Mr. Rush."

Mac furrowed her brow. "Did he go overseas?"

"I checked the foreign media. No sign of him there either." She passed the paper across the table to Mac. "As you can see, before, there is a plethora of information available about him and his career. I believe the man went to every gala and gave interviews to every reporter in New York City in the years before he dropped out of sight."

Yet another puzzle to be solved before they could make any headway. Mac felt like they were in a maze where every path led to a dead end. She needed a good pair of hedge clippers or better yet, a machete.

"You said a few things." Sam took the paper from Mac. "What else did you discover?"

"David Rush is not only an excellent painter, but he has many hobbies. One of which is collecting rare coins." Miss P drew out the last two words for emphasis.

Mac stopped writing and looked at her partners. "He was there when the time capsule was put together."

"But he was only eighteen." Sam frowned her disagreement.

"Yes, but he'd remember, and now that he's older, he'd know it's true worth."

"I guess." She pulled her hair away from her neck. "Is it hot in here?"

Being pregnant must be like having an internal heat source. "I'll turn the temp down." Mac stepped over to the thermostat on the wall.

Poor Miss P. She already wore a sweater to work. If things kept going like this, she'd need a jacket.

"Still, I believe Sam has a point," Miss P said. "I'm not sure Mr. Rush would remember the details of something that happened in high school, nor would he have known what other items were placed in the capsule. However, his aunt on his mother's side happened to be the head bank teller in charge of passing out the commemorative half dollars at the time."

"Is she still alive?"

"Oh, yes." Miss P removed her glasses and polished them with her handkerchief. "David Rush has been living with her since he moved back."

"Do we know what he looks like?"

"This is from about three years ago." Sam swiveled her computer around. "He did an interview for *Apollo*."

A full-page color photo of a slim, middle-aged man with a floppy brimmed hat and brown eyes. He stared into the camera from in front of an easel with a paint brush in one hand and a palette in the other.

"I had a feeling about the guy." Mac stabbed the air with her pencil. A cold breeze hit her neck like a warning of trouble yet to come.

"What guy?" Zoe's angry voice sounded at her back.

Mac slammed the computer and jumped out of her chair. She'd forgotten about Zoe. "I'm sorry, Zoe. I'm so used to driving myself—"

"I waited at your house for fifteen minutes. I called and texted." She stomped across the room. "Finally, I called Jake. He texted and called you."

"I didn't get any calls or texts." Mac retrieved her purse. No phone. She grabbed her keys and hurried out the door to her car. She'd left it on the charger.

As she scurried back to the office in the cold wind, she scrolled through the call register and the texts. Ouch. Jake was not happy with her.

Zoe looked up when she came in. She'd been crying. Mac swallowed a lump of guilt and pity for her former high school friend.

"Sam told me what you learned about David."

"I'm sorry, Zoe. I know you liked him."

"I still like him." She leaned forward over her cup of tea. "He may look bad on paper, but he's a great guy. I can't believe he would steal much less kill somebody."

"You may be right. It's early days."

Mac's phone rang. She pinched the bridge of her nose. If she didn't answer, he'd probably show up at the door. "Hi, Jake." She went into her office.

"Did Zoe find you?"

"Yes, she's here." Mac glanced at her closed door.

"And where is that?" His voice remained steely.

"The office." He started to answer, but she talked over him. "I'm sorry. I forgot. I'm used to being independent. It won't happen again."

The line hummed with silence. Had he hung up on her?

"Jake?"

"I'm here."

"I love you."

"I love you too. Leave your car at the office until I can follow you home."

"I will."

"See you later." Did he mean that as a threat or a promise? She laid her phone on the desk and joined the others.

"Something occurred to me while you were on your phone call." Miss P wrote with a graceful movement of her hand. "Do you have the list of men and women who were at the Downtown Merchants meeting the other night?"

"Why bother with that since the file was found?" Zoe pulled her sweater tighter. "Why is it so cold in here?"

Mac and Miss P exchanged a glance.

"The file was found in the copy room, correct? It's possible one of them made a copy."

"Good thinking, Miss P." Mac dug the piece of paper out of her folder.

"I'll make copies for each of us."

When she returned, Mac scanned the names. David Rush was fourth on the list. She glanced at Zoe.

A tear ran down her cheek.

CHAPTER 24

She drove him crazy. Jake stared at his phone. The woman did not understand he was trying to keep her safe. He ran a hand over his face. He knew what she would say to that.

"You expect me to support you in your job even though you put your life on the line every day. I have a job to do too. What's wrong with me expecting you to support me as well?"

And she'd be right. But why did she have to be a private investigator? Why not a librarian or a teacher? Scratch the teacher. That job was getting dangerous too. How about a writer? Yeah, the perfect job.

"You busy?" Vic leaned in through the open door.

Jake waved him in. "What's up?"

"I checked Owen's cellphone records." Vic offered him a sheet of paper. "There are calls to and from my Uncle Hank and Brandon Fischer—which I would expect." He came around to look over Jake's shoulder. "It's this number I wonder about. There're quite a few calls, and I think it's a burner phone."

"Who is this?" Jake tapped a highlighted number toward the bottom of the page.

"That's David Rush."

"Who's David Rush?"

"The artist. Moved to New York and became famous. Just moved back to open his own gallery."

"Oh yeah. Queenie told me about him." Jake rubbed his chin. "The call from Rush was an hour before Mac found Owen with his throat cut. I wonder what they talked about."

"You want me to find out?"

"Tell you what. Show your uncle the burner phone number and watch his reaction. See if he recognizes it." Jake closed the file on his desk. "I have something to take care of. I'll meet you back here in an hour. We'll go see Rush together."

"You got it."

Jake closed his door after Vic left and dialed Mac's number again. It went to voicemail. He didn't like the way their conversation ended. Even though they both declared their love, the mood was still tense.

He could text her he was sorry, but what was he sorry about? Not that he cared about her safety, or that he got upset when she put herself in harm's way. He laid his head back and closed his eyes. After she apologized, he should have eased up. That's what he felt bad about.

He called her again, but this time he left a message. "I don't blame you for not answering my call, Mac, and I'm sorry I talked to you like a detective instead of the man who loves you more than anything else in this world. I'll see you later."

Maybe he should go over to her office. He tapped his phone. Why didn't she return his call?

A knock and Vic slipped through the door. "Are you finished with whatever you needed to do?"

Jake nodded and pushed his phone to one side along with the heaviness in his spirit. He'd straighten it out later. For now, he had a job to do.

"Doesn't look like it went well for you either." Vic sank into the chair in front of Jake's desk. "No results on my end. Uncle Hank didn't recognize the phone number."

"Okay. Let's see what David Rush has to say."

"Where does he live?"

"His aunt has one of those condos on the river." Jake unlocked the SUV. "Across from Rennick Park."

"No kidding. That's where my uncle lives." Vic pulled Rush's cellphone records out of the file he carried. "There are a few calls between them, but that could be because he's leasing space in one of their buildings."

"That's the problem with a small town. Everybody knows everybody. It makes it hard to tell which connections are legitimate."

"I feel like I need a score card sometimes."

"What a view." Jake pulled to the curb in front of Six Front Street. A brick building housing eight three-story condominiums towered above him on his right. Rennick Park sloped down to the Missouri River on his left. Snow hung in the trees and covered the ground.

"Yeah," Vic said. "They're spectacular. His aunt must be loaded."

"What about your uncle?"

"He supposedly made money off his investments. We don't ask too many questions, and he doesn't offer much in the way of explanation."

Jake and Vic mounted the front stairs into the alcove. The door opened before they could ring the bell.

"If you're trying to save my soul, I'm afraid you're too late." A gray-haired woman in navy slacks and a fuchsia turtleneck sweater regarded them with one hand on her hip.

"No, ma'am. Those are the other guys." Jake held out his badge and ID.

"Police." Her penciled eyebrows rose. "This is a new one. Come in." She led them up a flight of stairs to the main living area. "Have a seat. Would you like something to drink?"

"No, ma'am." Jake eased himself onto a beige sofa facing the doors onto the balcony. Vic remained standing off to one side. "We really came to speak to your nephew, David Rush."

"In that case, you'll have to make another trip, I'm afraid." Her dangling earrings touched her shoulders as she shrugged. "He's in New York meeting with friends from the art world. He's hoping to drum up backers for his gallery here in Washington." She perched on the arm of a chair across from him. "I think he's a fool."

"Pretty harsh words for his only surviving relative." Jake studied the woman. Her driver's license said she was seventy-eight, but she didn't look it. The only signs were in her gray hair and her hands—the backs covered in brown spots and the knuckles swollen with arthritis.

"My nephew has talent, Detective Sanders, but he lacks business sense." She tapped the side of her head. "I refused to loan him the money he needs to open his gallery. Now he's gone begging to his friends. But I doubt that's what brought you here."

"No. We're following up on a call from his phone on the afternoon of January eleventh." Jake consulted his notes to make sure he had the date correct. "Would you know where your nephew was that afternoon?"

She rose and went into the kitchen to where a day planner lay on the kitchen counter. Vic eased over next to her. She pointed a lacquered nail to a notation under the date in question.

"David was here with me. I had some neighbors and friends over to introduce him." She closed the book. "A little afternoon affair."

"A social occasion?"

"Sort of." She sat and crossed her legs. "Just because I think he's a bad risk doesn't mean I won't help him try to get the backing he needs. He is my nephew after all."

"I see." What was the old saying? With friends like those who needs enemies? "I'll need a list of the other people at your party."

"Certainly." She left the room for a few minutes and returned with a pink piece of stationary that smelled faintly of roses. "I won't need this back."

Jake glanced at the list of names and frowned. "Charles Amory?"

"He has the end condo." Her bracelets jingled as she swept her arm to the right. "Henry Young lives here too. As does this couple." She pointed to two other names on the list. "What's the problem, Detective? Why are you so interested in David and my friends?"

"Thank you." He pushed to his feet. "When is your nephew expected to return?"

"He didn't give me a set day." She placed a hand on her hip. "You haven't answered my question."

Jake handed her his card. "I'd appreciate it if you'd call us when he gets back." He wasn't surprised when she didn't respond. "We'll see ourselves out." He paused at the top of the stairs to put on his coat and gloves.

In the alcove outside the door, Vic caught Jake by the arm. "I don't think she's going to let us know. She's—"

Jake silenced him with a look and strode down the walk to the street. In the car, he started the engine to get the heater working.

"She has a video doorbell. She could have heard anything we said on the porch." Jake moved the gearshift into drive and pressed the accelerator. "Did you get a look at the photographs on her bookcase?"

Vic nodded. "She has friends in high places. One showed her with the mayor."

"I'm talking about the ones of her and her nephew. David Rush has long dark blond hair. Wonder if he owns a mountain bike."

CHAPTER 25

A wave of compassion for Zoe mixed with thankfulness for Jake rushed through Mac. Her poor friend had fallen hard for the painter, and now it looked like he could be a thief and a murderer. Mac went in search of her phone.

She needed to call Jake and tell him how much she appreciated him, how she understood he was only trying to protect her, and how much she truly loved him. When she pressed the phone icon, a voicemail from Jake came up. It seemed he'd beat her to it.

The sound of his voice coupled with his words of apology left her knees weak. She plopped into her chair and supported her head with her hand. How had she come to deserve such a man?

"Knock, knock." Sam pushed her door open. "I think it's time to call Jake."

"I was just about to." Mac straightened and pressed one on her phone.

"Mac, glad you called. Vic and I are headed your way. We've got some news."

"We do too."

"Is Zoe with you?"

"Yes."

"Maybe you should send her home or on some errand."

Mac shared a look with Sam. "We suspect David Rush is involved, and she knows. I'm concerned she might tip him off. I think we should keep her here."

"You know about Rush?" There was a screech of tires, and a man's voice called, "Look out."

"Jake? Are you all right?"

"Yeah. Be there in ten."

"So, he knows about Rush too." Sam rubbed her stomach. "I wonder how."

"We'll know soon enough." Mac led the way back to the main room.

Miss P sat a plate of sandwiches on the table along with a bowl of potato chips and a pitcher of iced tea. "Not the healthiest of lunches, but it will have to do until I can get to the store."

Something wasn't right. Mac scanned the room. What was it? Her stomach dropped. No Zoe.

"Where's Zoe?" Mac prayed Miss P would say she was taking out the trash.

"She left."

Mac pinched the bridge of her nose. A dull pain throbbed between her eyes.

"Great." Sam threw her arms in the air. "She's gone to warn David Rush."

"I didn't think." Miss P looked stricken. "I should have stopped her."

"I doubt you could have." Mac put a hand on her friend's arm. "Besides, we don't know what she'll do." She picked up her phone. "I'll call her and see if I can't get her to come back."

Her call went to voicemail. "Zoe, remember who you're working for. Do not get in touch with David Rush."

Mac didn't hold out much hope when it came to work loyalties versus desires of the heart. She knew what she'd do if it were Jake.

"It's okay."

At the sound of Jake's voice, she pivoted to see him stomping snow off his boots. A smile sprung to her face, and she crossed the room to take his coat.

"Rush is in New York meeting with investors." He grinned at her. "Zoe probably won't be able to get in touch with him for a while."

"But she can leave a message." Vic hung up his coat and removed his boots.

"We'll have to catch him before he gets too far." Jake gave Mac a quick kiss on the cheek. "Time for show and tell." He urged her toward the conference table.

She stared at him. Jake never kissed her in public while on duty. Especially in front of his men. Vic could be considered more of a friend, but still. The press of Jake's hand on her back snapped her mind into focus. They had work to do. She grabbed a sandwich and sat in her usual spot.

"You go first." Jake poured a glass of iced tea. "What made you suspicious of Rush?"

"It was Miss P who got us started in that direction." Mac inclined her head at their researcher. "She realized the note Sam got was a crude clue directing us toward the painter."

Mac continued to report what Miss P found out about David Rush and finished by handing Jake the list of names of those present at the Downtown Merchants meeting. "Will you investigate those missing two years? We've done all we can." She looked at her notes. "And also, help us with the aunt?"

"We just came from the aunt's house," Vic said. "But I sure wish we'd known her background."

"We'll be going back." Jack nodded at the women. "You did good. This gives us a lot more to go on."

"So, what did you learn? Come on. Show and tell, remember?"

"We learned that while David Rush's aunt may love her nephew, she doesn't trust him with her money. She's not above helping him get money from her friends, however."

"Yeah." Jake swallowed a bite of his sandwich. "The day Owen Baker was killed, Rush was at a party his aunt was throwing to introduce him to her friends."

"Do you have a list of who was there?"

He pulled a pale pink paper from his pocket and handed it to her. She furrowed her brow as she read. Something seemed very familiar about the names. She reached for the list of people at the meeting in the library. They were the same. Except for one. Owen Baker either wasn't invited to David's aunt's house or hadn't come.

She placed both papers before Jake. "Could we be dealing with some sort of gang?"

"A group of retirees who got bored and decided to take up thievery?" Jake made a face at her.

"Or, a group of men and a woman who remembered the mule coin, know how much it's worth, decided to steal it, and split the money." Mac glared at him.

"I guess it's possible." He studied the list. "But I have a hard time with Brandon Fischer." He pointed to another name. "And what about Charles Amory? He's not from around here, and he came forward as a witness."

"True." She passed the pink paper to Miss P to copy.

"One thing more." Jake looked up from his notes. "We saw

some photos of Rush with his aunt. He has long dirty blond hair. Just like the guy on the bike."

Sam pulled on her ear. "But if that's the case, why didn't Mr. Amory recognize him when he met him at the aunt's party?"

Silence descended over the group of friends.

"Good question, sis. Another interview we need to follow up on." Jake made a notation on his pad. "What are you ladies going to do?"

"I have another idea I want us to pursue. I may need your help later." Mac stood and brushed breadcrumbs off her sweater. "And I need to get Zoe back here."

"Good idea." Jake moved in close. "Until this is over, you shouldn't go anywhere alone."

Mac was more interested in what her high school friend could tell them about her new boyfriend than making sure she had a ride, but she threw Jake a brief smile as if agreeing with him.

"That's a request. Not an order." He moved a few strands of hair off her face with his fingers. "I'm trying."

She caught his eyes with hers. "I love you." She spoke so only he could hear her words.

"Mackenzie, Zoe is on the line, and she wants to speak with you." Miss P held out the phone.

Jake backed away. "I'll call you later."

Mac lifted the phone to her ear as she watched Jake and Vic walk out the door. "Zoe? Where are you?"

"I had to get away. To think."

"I know it's tough, but we really need your help." Mac paced around the room. "We're not certain David has anything to do with the case, but you've talked to him. You know more about him than we can learn through newspaper articles or blogs. You could be the key to proving his innocence." Or guilt. But Mac wasn't going there.

"I called him. I got his voicemail, but I left a message." She drew in a breath. "Do you still want me to come back to the office?"

Mac rubbed her forehead. A dull ache had settled above her right eye. "Yes. Please. You're still a member of the team if you want to be."

"Okay. I'm on my way."

"Why would you want her back after she alerted our only suspect?" Sam glared at her.

"I have to admit I was wondering the same thing." Miss P peered at her over her glasses.

"Two reasons." Mac matched their looks with one of her own. "She has information we need. Like what does Rush look like now? Those photos could be old. Does he own a bicycle? Those kinds of things."

"What's the second reason?"

"You know the old saying? Keep your friends close and your enemies closer? If David Rush cares about Zoe—"

"He might come to us." Sam jumped up. "What a great idea. Let's lure the killer into our office. And what? We hit him over the head with a ream of copier paper?"

"No, that's not what I was thinking. I—"

"We call the police? Like that's turned out so well for us in the past." Sam marched over to her. "In case you've forgotten, I'm pregnant."

Mac's phone rang. Jake's face appeared on her screen. "Hold that thought. It's your brother."

"You'll never guess what happened." Excitement crackled in Jake's voice.

"Just tell me. You interrupted a serious discussion."

"David Rush walked into the police station and asked to see me."

CHAPTER 26

Mac pressed the speaker button on her phone. "What did you say?" She turned the volume up and motioned for Sam and Miss P to listen.

"I said, David Rush is here asking to see me." The shouted words echoed from the speaker. "Did you hear me that time?"

"Yes, thanks. Let me know what he has to say for himself."

"I will. Talk later."

Mac pushed End and sighed. "Can I finish what I was about to say now?"

Sam opened her mouth to speak.

"Samantha, stop being rude," Miss P said. "Give Mackenzie a chance to explain her reasoning."

Tears sprung to Sam's eyes, but she swiped them away and took her seat at the table.

A stab of pain hit Mac in her heart that matched the one over her eye. She hated seeing her friend hurt. But when she reached out to touch her hand, Sam moved it away.

"My thinking was that I didn't want another situation like

before and have David Rush smooth talk Zoe into helping with his plan." Mac massaged her forehead. "If she was with us, he wouldn't have a chance to involve her in his scheme. I couldn't stand the idea of another person I know being charged with a crime and put in jail. Not after our last case."

"He may have already convinced her to participate." Miss P removed her glasses and wiped the lenses with a special cloth. "In which case, her returning to us may be part of his plan. She may be a spy."

"To discover what we know?" Mac hadn't thought of that. "While he shows up at the police station to ..."

"Either throw them off course or discover what they know." Miss P replaced her glasses. "Or both."

"Either way, it's not safe to let her drive you around." Sam stared at her. "I'll do it."

"No." Mac gave an emphatic shake of her head. "If anything happened to you, I'd never forgive myself."

"Mackenzie Love, it's time you and everyone else stopped treating me like fine china." Sam pushed to her feet. "I don't even have a baby bump yet, and I'm a partner in this firm. It's time for me to act like a partner."

"You know your brother and your husband won't allow it."

"My brother has nothing to say about what I do, and my husband loves me. He trusts my decisions." She straightened. "Besides, I'm not a total idiot. I'll wear my bulletproof vest."

Mac grinned at her. "It's good to have you back, partner."

"What do we do with Zoe?" Miss P gave her a look. "You indicated she was still one of the team."

"Do you have any research left to do she could help with?"

"Yes. I think I can keep her busy for a time."

"Good." Mac got to her feet. "Sam, come with me." She led the way into her office. "I have this crazy idea Freddy hid the coin before turning over the things he stole from the time capsule."

"That's why Mr. Big is following you. He's using you to find it."

She nodded. "We need to find the coin without Mr. Big knowing about it. I want to meet with Tim Koenig again. He may have some idea where his brother might have hidden it."

"Okay. Let's get him into the office."

"Not with Zoe around." Mac chewed on her cuticle. "Let's go to him."

JAKE STEEPLED his hands in front of him. David Rush waited in Interview Room One, and he needed a game plan. "Vic, send Walker with some officers to execute search warrants on Rush's aunt's house and on his art gallery while we're talking to him."

"Do you think we have enough for a warrant?"

"It's thin, but I think so."

"Okay. Call as soon as you're finished." Vic pressed End. "They couldn't get warrants, but as the owner of the building, my uncle agreed to let them search the gallery. He's meeting them to unlock the doors."

"Is it legal?"

"Apparently, it's in the lease." Vic studied his notes. "How do you want to handle the Rush interview?"

"We'll start with easy questions. Name, when did he first know he wanted to be a painter, when did he move to New York. You get the picture." Jake jotted a few words on his pad. "Next get into the phone call and go from there."

The detectives rose and headed for the interview room. They checked the monitor before opening the door. A slim man dressed in a gray sweater, khakis, and boots paced the floor. His brownish blond hair was pulled back from his face into a bun at the back of his head. When he was farthest from the door, Jake pushed it open. Vic and another officer followed him in.

"Mr. Rush. Sit down." Jake waved a hand toward the chair facing the camera. "Please."

"I didn't do anything." David Rush advanced on Jake, his arms before him palms up.

He tensed. Was the man about to attack him or fall on his knees pleading for his life? "Sit down, Mr. Rush. No one has accused you of anything." Yet.

The man dropped his arms and did as he was told. He sat with his legs together and his hands folded in his lap. What was with this guy? He didn't act like a world-famous painter. He acted more like a ...

The missing two years. Jake scribbled a note and handed it to Vic, who gave a small nod and left the room. "Relax, Mr. Rush. We just need your help sorting out a few things about a case."

"What sort of things?" He raised dull green eyes to Jake.

"Would you like something to drink?"

"Some water?"

Jake pressed a number on his phone. "We need a water in here."

He made a show of studying his notes while assessing the man seated before him. Rush's hair and clothes looked clean and fresh, but dark shadows rimmed the lower lids of his eyes like he hadn't slept in days. What nightmares kept him awake at night?

There was a knock on the door, and the officer in the room retrieved the bottled water and handed it to Rush. The painter removed the cap and took a long drink.

"Why don't we start with your full name and age for the record."

"David Arthur Rush. Fifty-two."

Jake eyed him. He looked younger than fifty-two and acted way younger. "You grew up in Washington, right?"

"Yes."

"Did you like it here? Was it a good place to live?"

"Yes and yes."

Sparks of frustration threatened to set fire to Jake's well-constructed plan for this interview. "When did you start painting?"

Rush held up a hand. "Detective Sanders, I don't mean to be disrespectful, but my aunt told me you wanted to know about a call I made to Owen—Mr. Baker on the day he died." He leaned forward. "I never phoned Owen. I was at my aunt's house all day meeting her neighbors and friends, and I didn't make any phone calls. In fact, I left my phone in my room on purpose so I wouldn't be distracted."

"Who had access to your room?"

"I guess anyone could have walked in there."

"Is your phone password protected?"

"Yes. Of course."

"Who knows the password?"

"Only me." A shadow passed over his face.

"You're sure?"

He nodded.

"So how do you explain the call from your phone on Owen Baker's call records two hours before he was killed?"

"I can't." His eyes seemed to sink back under the shadow of his brow. "All I know is it wasn't me." Rush pulled his phone from his pocket, tapped a few keys, and handed it to Jake. "See for yourself. I didn't call Owen Baker."

Jake searched the call log. It wasn't there. "We'll need to keep this for a while."

The man sagged in his chair. "Of course."

There was a knock on the door, and Vic entered the room. He handed a piece of paper to Jake. Now they knew where David Rush had been the two years before moving to Washington, Missouri. In prison.

CHAPTER 27

"We're going to take a break, Mr. Rush. Don't go anywhere." Jake nodded to the officer at the back of the room and stepped into the hall with Vic. "This changes things."

"Now we know why he came back to Washington." Vic tapped his phone. "His career took a nosedive."

"It says here fraud. Any details?"

"He forged a couple of checks." Vic flipped through a file. "He was working with someone, but he refused to give up the name of his partner. Since it was his first offense, they went light on him. Two years. Minimum security."

"Forging checks doesn't usually translate into robbery and murder." Jake ran a hand through his hair. "Let's see what he has to say for himself." He led the way through the door into the interview room. "Mr. Rush, does your aunt know you were in prison?"

He stiffened, and the color drained from his face. "Please don't tell her."

"What happened? I thought you were doing so well."

"I was. For a time." Rush rubbed his forehead. "I got into debt and needed a way out."

"So, you thought it would be a good idea to steal money by forging the signatures of a couple of your wealthy clients."

"I altered their checks to show a larger purchase price. I figured they wouldn't notice, and they had the money."

"What you didn't count on is rich people pay very close attention to every penny. It's how they got where they are."

"Yes."

"But there's more to the story. You had a partner. Who was it?"

He averted his gaze. "No partner. Only me."

No sense pushing it. That wasn't why they were here. "You moved back to Washington in order to what? Lie low for a while? Get your career back on track? What?"

"All those things. I'm still a good painter. It's what I do." He raised his face to look Jake squarely in the eyes.

"Someone matching your description was seen leaving the scene shortly after the murder two days ago."

"It wasn't me." He jumped to his feet and took a step toward Jake. "I doctored a couple of checks, but I would never kill someone."

"Sit down, Mr. Rush." Jake glared at him.

Vic and the other officer moved closer to Rush.

The tall man lowered himself to the chair once more, his once pale face flushed and his breathing became rapid.

"Take a drink and calm down, Mr. Rush."

He did as he was told. Jake read through his notes and glanced at the man sitting across from him. He was convincing, but many suspects could be.

"You were around when the sesquicentennial time capsule was put together. What do you remember about it?"

"I was a kid." He glanced at Jake. "I remember winning a

contest, and my drawing was put in the thing." He gulped some more water. "I think my aunt had something to do with it, but I'm not sure what."

"She never talked to you about it? Not even since you've been back?"

"Not until recently when it got broken into."

"What did she say about it? Recently, I mean."

"She said it was sad to think some unruly teenagers had nothing better to do than destroy a public landmark." He gave Jake a curious look. "Why?"

"Nothing about its contents?"

"No. I'm not sure she remembers. She is seventy-eight."

Jake threw a look at Vic. The woman they met had a mind as sharp as a chef's knife.

Vic's phone buzzed, and Jake gave him an annoyed look. Until Vic passed it to him to read. The search of David Rush's rental space turned up a bicycle saddle bag holding the plans for the city and the parks among other things. But no silver half dollar.

"Do you own a bicycle, Mr. Rush?" Vic asked.

"What does that have to do with anything?" He threw his hands up in a show of exasperation.

"Answer the question." Jake didn't move. His tone was enough. David Rush sat up straight and folded his hands once more.

"Yes, sir."

"Where is it?"

"At my aunt's house."

"Describe it."

"It's a mountain bike." Rush looked at Jake as if trying to figure out what he wanted. "Black? With a saddlebag on the back fender?"

"When did you last ride it?"

"I don't remember." Sweat beaded on Rush's forehead.

"Try."

The man closed his eyes. "A week ago? Maybe? I've been driving everywhere lately."

"What kind of car do you own?"

"A Toyota Corolla."

Vic handed his phone to Jake. David Rush owned a red 2021 Toyota Corolla.

Jake gave him a sharp glance before making a note. "While we've been speaking, I had a few men searching the space you've leased for your new gallery." Jake studied the man for his reaction. A flash of what seemed to be anger passed across his face, but nothing else. "We found your saddlebag. It contained most of the items from the time capsule."

"That's not possible." Rush sprang to his feet. "I didn't—"

Jake pushed to his feet. "David Rush, I'm arresting you on suspicion of destroying public property, theft of public property, and of murder." Jake pointed behind him. "This officer will read you your rights."

"I didn't do anything."

The man was screaming now.

"Listen to me. I'm innocent. I'm being framed."

Jake and Vic closed the door and walked down the hall to Jake's office. A heaviness settled over Jake. Something in his spirit told him he was making a mistake.

CHAPTER 28

Excitement coursed through Mac's veins, and she found it hard to sit still. She and Sam had an appointment to see Tim Koenig in an hour at the Meerschaum Pipe Museum. They should leave early to make certain they weren't followed, but were they skilled enough to lose a tail? Probably not.

Jake was interviewing David Rush, and she itched to text him and find out how it was going. But she knew he wouldn't answer.

Was David Rush Mr. Big? Or was he merely another pawn in the game? She glanced at the clock for the hundredth time. In five minutes, she'd get her partner, and they'd leave.

The door to her office opened, and Sam popped her head in. "Ready to go? I can't stand waiting any longer."

"We'll take our time." Mac clicked her buckle in place. "Go around the block a time or two to see if any cars appear to be following us."

"I plan on taking a circuitous route. Keep your eyes peeled." Sam stretched the belt across and struggled to get it fastened. "I forgot how bulky and uncomfortable these vests are."

"I'm sorry I got us into this situation." Mac shook her head.

"You can't help it." Sam patted her arm. "Trouble follows you around, my friend. I've resigned myself to it."

"Great." Mac cringed. "That makes me feel a whole lot better."

"I'd rather be wearing this thing and be with you than back at the office constantly worried about you. At least now I feel like I can do something."

"And I'm more thankful for that than I can say." Mac kept glancing in the side mirror and out the windows. No cars seemed to be following them. "I think we're clear." Her phone rang, and she pressed the green button without looking at her screen. "Mackenzie Love."

"I thought I was supposed to drive you around."

Uh-oh. Zoe, and she was not happy.

"You hired me to be your sidekick. You said I was still part of the team."

"I did, and you are. I needed to talk to a guy, and Sam wanted to get out of the office for a while." She cut her eyes to Sam, who stared straight ahead. "Besides, Miss P can use your help. We'll be back soon."

"What guy? Where are you going?"

"I've got another call. We'll talk later." Mac buzzed over to Jake and put it on speaker. "You saved me from the wrath of Zoe."

"What?"

"Never mind. How did your interview go?"

"There's a lot of evidence that points to him."

"Like what?"

"We found the contents from the time capsule still in the saddlebags in Rush's rented space downtown."

Sam pulled to the curb and stopped the car. "Were they sitting in plain sight?"

"No, hidden behind some pipes in the utility room, but I know, it seems too easy."

"It does." Mac furrowed her brow. "What else did you find out?"

"He owns a black mountain bike. The guys are on their way over to the aunt's house with a warrant now. And he drives a red car."

"Like the one that's been following me?" Her right hand tightened into a fist. Maybe he wasn't Mr. Big, but he could be working for him.

"Rush protested his innocence all the way through to the end. To tell you the truth, I've got a feeling he may be telling the truth."

"Or he's as good an actor as he is a painter." Facts swirled around in her mind. She squeezed her eyes shut and prayed for clarity. What did it all mean?

"You could be right."

"Was the coin with the things you found in his saddlebags?" If it was, her whole idea about the case was false.

"No."

She let out the breath she'd been holding. Mr. Big, whoever he was, would still be looking for the coin. And she had to beat him to it. The race was on.

"Anything else I should know?"

"Oh, the two-year gap in his history. He was in prison for forging checks."

Mac shared a why-hadn't-we-thought-of-that look with Sam. "Thanks, Jake. Talk later."

"Wait. Where are you, and what are you doing?"

"Sam and I are about to meet up with Tim Koenig to see if he can help us figure out where his brother might have hidden the half-dollar."

"Sam?"

Mac held the phone at arm's length.

"Samantha, what do you think you're doing? Don't move. I'm coming."

"Don't you dare, Jake Sanders." Sam used her sternest voice. "I am a grown woman and can make my own decisions. Besides, I'm not stupid. I'm wearing my vest."

"You call me every half hour to check in or—"

"I will not call you every half hour, but I will let you know how things are going. Now we have an appointment. Good-bye, bro." Sam pressed End.

Mac grinned at her. "You'll make a great mother. You already have the tone of voice down."

Sam smiled and started the car. She waited for a green panel van and a white four-door sedan to pass before pulling onto the street. "I guess we don't have to watch for a tail?"

"If there is one, I haven't spotted it. I was looking for the red car."

"Me too." Sam turned onto Cedar Street. "There's the Meerschaum pipe museum."

"Looks like we have our pick of parking spaces. Nobody's here."

"At least they cleared the snow off the street."

Mac held Sam's arm as they crossed the street. Last thing they needed was for her to fall. Someone had taken care of the deck and stairs. The damp wood shone in the weak January sun.

Mac tried the door. Locked. She knocked and pressed her face to the glass. Nobody there. Where was Tim? Her pulse sped up. Could he be the next victim of Mr. Big? She pulled her phone from her pocket and had her finger on the call button when he appeared from the back. A sigh of relief escaped her.

"You had me worried. I thought you'd changed your mind

about meeting us." Or been hurt. But she stopped herself before those words came out of her mouth.

"Nay. I saw a guy come up to the door and didn't want him to see me. People do that all the time thinking I'll let them in for a minute to look around. Like the hours posted on the door aren't meant for them."

"I can imagine," Sam said. "Would you rather we talk in the car? Or at a restaurant?"

"Well, I am hungry."

"Let's go across the street to underGrounds Expresso Bar."

"Great. I'm addicted to their frittatas." He rubbed his hands together. "And their coffee is the best."

Irregular piles of dirty snow edged the street, and once again, Mac held onto Sam as they made their way across to the restaurant. As the name implied, steps led down to the door. Yet another chance for a fall. Who knew caring for her pregnant partner was going to be so full of little dangers?

When they stepped inside, Mac let out the breath she'd been holding. She spied two unoccupied leather wing chairs under a brick arch and headed for them. "Get me a latte, Sam. You know how I like it. I'll save us some seats." She grabbed a silver chair with a green pillow to make room for three.

While waiting for Sam and Tim, she surveyed the room. Several tables were occupied. Mostly by couples with two singles. All were glued to their phones except the slim woman sitting closest to them who glanced from her watch to the door.

She wore leather boots over skinny jeans and a bright pink puffy jacket. A pink knit cap with a bobble on top was pulled tight over her head. Mac mistook her for a young girl until she raised her cup to her mouth. Her hands were the veined hands of an older woman.

A man pushed through the door bundled up to his head,

his face covered by a navy scarf. He went to the counter and placed his order.

"I'll sit on the metal chair." Tim arranged the chair so he could use the wood chunk nearby as his table and took a bite of his sandwich. "Hmmm."

Sam handed Mac a drink and eased herself into one of the wing chairs.

The man at the counter collected his coffee and came over to the woman's table. He pecked her on the cheek and sat across from her. Mac squinted at him.

"It's not polite to stare." Sam nudged her.

"Can you make out what's in his ear?"

"It's an ear bud, goofy. Where have you been for the last decade? You should get a set, and your phone wouldn't sound off in public."

"Do you have a pair?"

"Yes. I thought you'd seen me with them on."

Mac sighed. She let her eyes close for a second and imagined she and her partner weren't there for business, but just for fun. A girl's day out. Shopping maybe. It had been so long since she and Sam had taken a day for fun, she couldn't remember it. "Do you remember us ever going shopping together?"

Sam scrunched her face. "Maybe for business furniture?"

"Sad." Mac shook her head. "We need to take a girls' day."

"I agree." Sam put her cup on the table between them. "But now, we have work to do. Tim, we need your help."

"You said that on the phone." He shook his head back and forth several times. "But I've told the police all I know."

"This is different." Mac leaned forward. "We believe Freddy hid something before he met with Mr. Big. That's what I call his killer, the guy who hired him, and got him into this mess. I think it's small. About like this." She made a circle with her fingers about the size of the half dollar. "Where would he hide it?"

"I told you and the police, I haven't had any contact with my brother for years." He leaned back in his chair. "How should I know?"

"You grew up together. People don't change much. Think, please."

He dropped his head into his hands. After a moment, he straightened, and his mouth opened as if to speak. He raised his eyes to Mac. "What was he driving?"

"A dark-colored SUV."

"When we were kids, our dad had a van. In the back, there was a small cover where some kind of accessory could be added. Course, we didn't know that at the time. We pried it off and stashed things in there. We called it our hiding place."

Adrenaline pulsed through her, and she was eager to be done with the interview. She squirmed in her chair.

"Great, Tim. Any other places you can think of?" Sam threw Mac a cool-it look.

The man at the table near them stood, pulling her attention away from what Tim was saying. He kissed the woman, and as he walked away, Mac noticed he had a slight limp.

Sam nudged her again.

"Not off hand, but I'll think about it some more and give you a call."

"Thanks, Tim." Mac stood. "You can stay, but we need to be going."

"I'm ready too."

On the sidewalk outside the restaurant, Mac shook hands with Tim while Sam gave him a hug.

"Thanks again. You've been a big help."

"Let me know if you find anything, okay?" He hunched his shoulders against the cold wind that swirled around them.

"We will. We're up here." Mac inclined her head up the sidewalk. "Talk to you later." She and Sam hurried up the sidewalk toward their car as Tim stepped off the curb to cross the street.

A green panel van barreled around the corner.

CHAPTER 29

The front end of the van clipped Tim and sent him spinning. He crumpled to the street. "Call 911." Mac raced to the twisted body lying on the wet pavement. "Tim, can you hear me? Don't try to move. Help is on the way."

"Shmm mn."

"I can't understand you. It's okay. Don't try to speak."

He drew in a tortured breath and caught Mac's eyes with his. "Shame minn."

"Same man?" She understood with a terrible suddenness. "The same man who came to your door earlier?"

Tim gave a slight nod and closed his eyes.

"Move." The EMT shoved her aside.

She'd been concentrating so hard on what Tim was trying to say she hadn't heard the ambulance arrive. She backed away and did the only thing left for her to do—pray.

Sam took her by the arm and led her to the car. "Let's sit inside until they're done. I called Jake."

"Tim said it was the same man who came to the museum before we got there." She stared out the window to where emergency personnel were lifting Tim onto a stretcher. "Which means whoever it is, tried to kill him before we could talk to him. But why? If Mr. Big wants us to find the coin, you'd think he wouldn't interfere with us."

"Maybe there's something else Tim knows that the killer was afraid we'd find out."

"Like his identity." She took a quick breath of utter astonishment. Could Tim know who his brother's killer was without realizing it?

As Jake turned onto Cedar Street, his eyes were drawn to the dark patch on the concrete where Tim had fallen, and a sudden chill squeezed his heart like a vise. It could have been Mac or Sam. A fierce desire to protect them raged within him, but there was no way he could, nor would they let him. He caught sight of them sitting in Sam's car and whispered a prayer of thanks for their safety.

Sam rolled down her window. "It's about time you got here."

Another patrol car rolled up behind him, drowning out his rude answer. Which was for the best.

"I'm here now. Unlock the doors. I'll sit with you." Jake approached the other police officers. "Take pictures and measurements. I'll get statements."

His sister usually kept her car at sauna temperature, but today, it was almost as cold as outside. Mac still had her coat and gloves on while Sam sat in short sleeves. "Sis, could you bump up the heat?"

"I guess." She raised it a couple of degrees.

Mac mouthed "thank you" to him over the seat.

"So, what happened today?" Jake took out his notepad. Like Mac, he still liked to write things down.

"This was supposed to be a simple meeting with Tim Koenig to get help about where Freddy might have hidden the coin." Mac swiveled so she could see Jake. "And it was. Until we got ready to leave. He started across the road, and the van came out of nowhere."

"Any details about the van?"

"It was a green panel van."

"I think it was the same one we saw earlier." Sam caught her brother's eyes in the rearview mirror. "We had finished talking to you, and I was pulling away from the curb. A green van with a logo passed us."

"You remember what it said?"

"Something plumbing." Sam squeezed her eyes shut. "What are the tractors that are green?"

"Wouldn't know." Jake shook his head.

"Deer Plumbing. That's it."

"I'm impressed, sis." He smiled at her in the mirror. She was paying attention to her surroundings. He felt a lot more at ease.

"Jake, we need to get a look at Freddy's SUV," Mac said.

"Why?"

"I think he hid the coin in there."

"Our guys inspected every inch. If the mule coin was there, they would have found it."

"Not if it was hidden in a special place." Mac grinned at him. "Please."

Jake regarded the beautiful face of his girlfriend. Her chestnut brown eyes shown with anticipation and the assurance she was on to something. Her excitement was infectious. Why not? What could it hurt?

"Okay, but I go with you."

"Of course. Where is it?"

Mac and Sam followed him to the impound lot, where Jake flashed his badge to get them inside. The navy-blue SUV sat all alone at the back of the lot.

"Do we need gloves?" Sam asked.

Jake shook his head. "They're done with it."

"Have you got a pocketknife on you?" Mac held out her hand.

"What do you want with that?"

"I'm not going to slice up the upholstery." She eyed the interior. "Any worse than it is already. I need it to pry open a panel."

"Now you have my attention." He knew what she was talking about, but he'd never tried to remove one.

"Tim said they used to hide things behind a small panel in their dad's van. I want to see if there's a place like that in Freddy's SUV." She slid in on the driver's side while Sam climbed in on the passenger side.

Jake stooped next to Mac as she and Sam examined the dashboard. Nothing looked promising. Mac probed a few places, but with no results. He followed her gaze to the controls for the interior lights and two of the lights themselves located on the ceiling between the front two seats. In the middle of the switches was a rectangular piece the same color as the headliner. Mac found an edge with the knife blade and gave it a gentle twist.

The piece popped off, and something shiny flew out and clattered to the floor between Sam's feet. She gasped.

"We found it." Mac stared at the mule half dollar in amazement.

Jake jogged around the car to Sam's side and opened her door. He took a glove from his pocket, retrieved the coin from the floor, and held it to the light. "Wow." He flipped open an evidence bag and dropped it inside. "Nice one, ladies. Wait till the guys hear about this."

Mac jumped from the SUV and joined him. "It doesn't help you find out who's behind all this." She reached for the baggie and examined the silver coin inside. "But at least we now have the motive in hand."

"I do, and that means a lot." He took it back and tucked it inside his jacket. "Now it's back to the precinct. We'll talk later."

"We're coming with you. We need to see the rest of the items taken from the capsule." Mac stood squarely in front of him. "We have a case to finish and a client to satisfy."

"Yeah. I forgot." He pressed his lips together. "Follow me back."

Jake wanted to keep the recovery of the stolen memorabilia quiet for a while longer. When Hank Young found out about it, the whole town would know within hours. He glanced in his mirror as Sam backed out of her space. He signaled for a right turn and pressed the accelerator. Maybe he could convince them to hold off telling Young for a couple of days.

He pushed a button on his steering wheel. "Call the precinct." When the call connected, he asked for the Chief.

"Where are you?"

"Leaving the impound. It's a long story. I found the coin— well, Mac and Sam found the coin."

"Get in here. Pronto."

"I'm on my way." A flash of green in his rearview mirror captured his attention. "No. No. No." He slammed on the brakes.

CHAPTER 30

"I may strangle your brother." Mac growled through her teeth at the black SUV already half a block away.

"You'll have to get in line." Sam turned right out of the parking lot. "Follow me."

Sam did a good imitation of Jake, and Mac barked a laugh. "You're—Look out!"

The green panel van roared at them from the left.

Mac pitched forward against her seatbelt as Sam slammed on the brakes. The SUV swerved to the right as the back fishtailed before coming to a stop parallel with the van.

The tinted passenger window in the van began a slow descent.

"Go. Go. Go." Mac swatted Sam on the arm.

Sam hit the accelerator. The tires spun before gaining purchase and launching them back into their seats. Thankfully, the airbags hadn't deployed.

The driver of the van was slower to react, which gave them a slight advantage.

"Where do we go?" Sam hunched over the steering wheel.

"At the junction, take a right." Mac glanced over her shoulder. "He's back there, but he's not gaining on us."

Sam swerved to her left.

"What are you doing? I told you to take a right."

"This is right."

"No, this is left." Mac pressed her fingers to her temples. What was on this road? The cement factory?

"I'm an idiot." Sam slapped her palm on the wheel. "He's going to kill us." She rubbed her stomach. "It's all my fault."

"Sam. Stop." Mac shook her. "We're not dead yet. I'll call Jake."

No reception. She tossed the phone on the dash. "Never mind. Jake will figure out we're not behind him and come back. Besides, we're private investigators. We have skills. That's what you always tell me."

"And you believe me?" she gave a hysterical laugh.

"Stop it." Mac's words snapped through the air like a whip, but they had the desired effect.

Sam shot her a glare.

"I need your help if we're going to get out of this."

"I'm driving as fast as I can."

"Does this thing have four-wheel drive?"

"I think so. There's a button somewhere." Sam took her focus off the road to look for the button.

"Don't. You drive. I'll look."

One button had squiggly lines on it, and another seemed to be a schematic of the underside of the car. Could one of those be it? *Lord, I need your help.* Then she saw it—a square button to the left of the gear shift marked FWD.

"I found it." She twisted around to look out the back. The van was gaining on them. "Do you remember where we found the truck that crashed into me last year?"

"Kind of."

"We're heading back there."

"Are you crazy?" Sam cut her eyes toward Mac. "It's not even a road."

"We have four-wheel drive. We don't need a road."

"But it's been snowing. It'll be impossible."

"We can do it. We have high clearance and traction." Mac prayed she sounded more certain than she felt. But she couldn't see any other hope for them. "You didn't, by chance, bring your gun?"

"No. Did you?"

"No." Mac pushed the four-wheel-drive button. "Take the track on the right. Your other right this time."

Sam gunned the motor and hit the snow-covered path at full speed. The SUV slid sideways before the tires found traction and took off. She gripped the steering wheel as they bounced over the rutted road.

Mac placed one hand on the ceiling and the other wrapped around her seatbelt as she tried desperately to see whether the man in the green van would come after them.

The SUV jolted to a stop. They'd hit deep snow.

"We need to get out and run." Mac struggled to undo her seatbelt. Why weren't her fingers working? "Sam, go. Get out of here."

"I'm not leaving without you." Sam reached over and pressed the release on Mac's belt. It sprung open.

The two women jumped out, the snow up to their knees. "Sam, grab the bars on top. Get to the back." Mac grabbed the luggage rack on top of the SUV and pulled herself out of the drift.

"We need to hide." Mac scanned the trees to their left. "Beyond the woods is Dubois Creek. It might be frozen enough to cross." Mac pushed through the snow, aware her tracks would be easy to follow. She prayed once among the trees the snow would be sparse and they would find a place to hide. Or better yet be able to cross the creek.

As they entered the woods, Mac spied the van. Vapor billowed from the exhaust as it idled at the beginning of the lane. Was the driver out here somewhere hunting for them? She pulled Sam into a crouch. "He could be out here," she said in a low voice.

Blood pounded in her ears. Would she be able to hear the crunch of his boots? Her body trembled from the cold. Even her eyeballs felt frozen. How could she defend herself or Sam? And the baby. Her heart lurched in her chest.

She turned to her friend. Sam rocked gently on her knees, murmuring to herself. What was she saying? Mac leaned down.

"The Lord is my strength and my shield. My heart trusts in Him." Sam repeated the verse from Psalms over and over.

Mac joined in her whispered prayer.

An engine revved and tires squealed. Mac looked out in time to see the green van speed off in the direction they'd come. While the sweet sound of a siren filled the air.

"Sam, get up. Jake's here." Mac pulled Sam to her feet, and they slogged through the snow to the trail.

Jake's police SUV sped past the beginning of the lane, siren blasting.

"Come on." Mac trudged toward the street. "He'll be back."

"How do you know?"

"It's a dead end. Once he figures out we're not down there, he'll come back looking for us."

Sam draped an arm over Mac's shoulders. "See, I was right."

"About what?"

"When I told you we'd be all right. We're private investigators. We have skills."

Mac growled at her. "If you weren't pregnant, I'd elbow you in the stomach."

"Now, now, Auntie Mac. Baby can hear everything you say."

Auntie Mac, again. A surge of emotion left a lump in her throat. Would she ever get to be Mommy? She shook herself. No sense thinking about that right now. Reflections of blue and red danced on the snow before Jake's SUV came into view.

"Over here." They called out to him and waved.

He threw the door open, leaped through the snow, and wrapped both women in a bear hug. A gust of icy air hit them, and Mac's whole body shivered. The adrenaline rush had masked the cold up till now.

"Get in my car while I retrieve your things." Jake gave them a gentle shove in the direction of the street.

After a few feet, Mac turned. "Jake, my phone is on the passenger side dash."

He gave her a thumbs up.

The crack of a shot echoed off the trees.

CHAPTER 31

As Jake watched Mackenzie and his sister fall to the ground, agony roared through him and out his mouth. He yanked his pistol from its holster and held it against his chest. Rage threatened to override his training, and it was all he could do not to empty his gun into the woods. If he could get a fix on the shooter, he'd return fire, but otherwise, he was helpless.

Flashing lights and a howling siren announced the arrival of a squad car. Jake ran as fast as he could through the snow to where the women lay face down.

"Are you hurt?" He dropped beside them.

"I'm not." Mac pushed to her knees.

"Stay down." Jake pressed her back onto her stomach and turned to his sister. "Samantha?"

She spit out some snow and grass. "I'm okay. But this is not the most comfortable position for a pregnant woman."

"Better than dead." Jake whistled at the officers by the squad car and motioned for them to move into the woods from their end. "I'll be back."

He squatted beside them and watched as his men hurried into the trees, guns drawn. Time to move. Keeping low, he bulldozed over the uneven ground and through the drifts of snow until he reached the woods.

Back against a tree, he paused to let his heart rate decrease and his eyes and ears adjust to the low light and the silence of the woods. His men would be headed toward him. He needed to alert them of his presence.

"Clear on this end." A flock of birds took flight from a nearby bush.

"Clear on this end." One of his officers called out.

Jake swung out from behind the tree in a semi crouch, his gun held out in front of him. "Washington Police. Show yourself." No telltale sounds of movement and no one in sight.

He moved forward to another large tree. He heard his men announcing themselves. They were much closer than before. Well past where the shooter should have been. "Stay put. I'm coming your way."

"Copy that."

His instinct told him the gunman had escaped. Still, he knew better than to let his guard down. He studied each shadow with care until he caught sight of the dark uniforms of his men among the trees.

"I think we found where he shot from," one of the officers said.

"Show me."

The officer led him to a patch of trampled snow by a pine tree. Jake studied the ground. No footprints or cigarette butts to use as evidence. But a branch sticking out from the tree was at just the right height to rest a rifle on for the shot, and it bore scratch marks. He lifted his arms as if he held a rifle.

It would have been an easy shot. Assuming the guy was aiming for Mac, how had he missed her? Even if she moved at the last minute, the bullet should have caught her in the side or the arm. Instead, it went right between her and Sam. Almost as if ...

He intended to miss.

Jake dropped his arms and realized what he was seeing beyond the woods. Or rather not seeing. No Mac and Sam. He stepped over a mound of snow and stood at the edge of the trees. Where were they? His phone vibrated in his pocket. It was Sam. "I thought I told you to stay put."

"We did. Until we started to get frostbite on our fingers and toes."

"Where are you?" He scanned the view before him, but in the late afternoon shadows, he couldn't pick out the two women.

"We got our purses from my SUV, and now we're sitting in your police car waiting on you. How much longer are you going to be? We're freezing, and we're starved."

He relaxed his grip on his phone. "Five or ten minutes. There're some blankets in the back."

"This is no way to treat a pregnant lady, bro."

Jake rolled his eyes. "I get it, sis." He turned away from the site and continued his search. Three feet from where the gunman stood was a boot print in the snow.

"Get forensics out here right away." More indentations led toward the creek. Jake turned to the officer next to him. "Show forensics the footprints to cast and take pictures. Oh, and search for the shooter's shell casing."

"Yes, sir."

"I'm taking Mac and Sam back to the precinct. We'll talk later."

The temperature inside his SUV was only a few degrees warmer than outside. "Sorry you guys had to be out in the cold so long."

"Start the car. We need heat." Sam bumped the temperature up as high as it would go.

Jake glanced at his sister huddled in the passenger seat. Her teeth were chattering. In the rearview mirror, Mac appeared to be studying her phone. He pulled around the police car and headed for the station.

A few minutes later, Sam shed her blanket, her jacket, and she'd turned the heat to air conditioning. Jake shook his head.

A sharp intake of breath came from the back seat.

"What's wrong, Mac?" He peered into his mirror at her.

"I got another text."

"What does it say?" Sam swiveled in her seat to look back at her friend.

"You have what I want. Give it to me, or next time I won't miss, and your friend will die." Mac lifted a pale face to Sam. "What have I done?"

"Nothing." Sam spoke in a stern voice. "Mr. Big is the bad guy, not you." She placed a hand on her stomach. "I'm sure Jake can provide me with all the protection I need. Right, bro?"

He looked in the rearview mirror at Mac. Their eyes met in a silent understanding. They would protect Sam at all costs. "I'll move in with you and Alan if that's what it takes."

"Killer would love it, but I'm not so sure I would." Sam made a sound halfway between a chuckle and a snort.

Mac caught his eyes in the rearview mirror once more. "I need the coin back."

His hands clenched the steering wheel as he realized what she was planning. "Don't even think about it."

"It's the only way we'll catch this jerk."

"What are you two talking about?" Sam asked, her voice shrill with anxiety.

"Mac wants to arrange a meeting with Mr. Big to give him the coin."

"No way. That's suicide." Sam pivoted to look at her. "I forbid it."

As Jake pulled into the parking lot, he caught a glimpse of Mac's stony face, and the blood in his veins felt like cold needles. He ushered them into the elevator this time, none of them up to the climb to the second floor.

As they entered Jake's office, Alan grabbed Sam in a warm hug. "Baby doll. I couldn't stand to be at work, so I came here to wait."

Sam lit up at the endearment. "Alan, hush. I'm fine." She placed a hand on his cheek.

Jake's gaze went to Mac. Lines of guilt and regret were etched on her face, and he wanted more than anything to smooth them away with his kisses.

"I'm so glad to see you both unharmed." Miss P stepped out of the corner of the room. "Let's keep it that way, shall we? I too felt led to wait at the station for your return, and since we're all here, I suggest we put our heads together and try to figure out who's the real Mr. Big."

"Good idea. We'll use the conference room down the hall." Jake led the way. "Take a seat. I'll be back."

He returned with Detective Victor Young, and notepads, pencils, and water for everyone. "Where should we start?"

"David Rush." Vic tapped his pencil on his pad. "After what happened to you guys this afternoon, it looks like he's in the clear."

"Maybe." Jake pulled at his ear. His instinct told him Rush was involved somehow. "Or the shooter works for him. Or vice versa."

"Or he's framing Rush."

"If that's the case, he'd have to have access to his phone."

"True." Vic scratched something out on his pad.

"I believe the shooter and the man in the green van are the same. Don't you?" Mac asked.

Jake and Sam nodded.

"Maybe we should go back to our visit to Tim Koenig and tell you what happened first." Mac said. "You may see something we didn't."

"Okay." Jake sat back. "Although I think Koenig was an accident. He was aiming for you.

Mac shook her head. "I was on the sidewalk."

"Maybe he was looking at you and didn't notice Koenig."

"I guess, but that's not the impression I got." Mac held up a hand. "But let me tell you about our visit." She described their interview from their brief time in the museum to deciding to go to the underGrounds Expresso Bar.

When she got to the part about the woman, Vic held up a hand. "Whoa. You said she had bangles on her wrists, but the hands of an older woman?"

"Yes, but she was slim and moved like a much younger one."

"Did she have short gray hair?"

"I couldn't really tell. It was covered by her knit cap." Mac furrowed her brow. "But come to think of it, her bangs were light. They could have been white or gray."

Vic pulled up a photo of David Rush's aunt and showed it to Mac. "Is this her?"

"It could be." Mac examined the photo. "Yes, it definitely could be her."

"Tell us about the man."

She described the man, but he was so bundled up there weren't many details to go on. Jake stopped doodling on his pad. David Rush would know if his aunt was seeing someone. He pulled his phone from his pocket and indicated he needed a moment.

"Walker, I need you to do something. Go ask Rush if his aunt is dating anyone, and if so, who is it. Also, see if his aunt knows the password to his phone. Thanks."

"Rush is here? I thought you charged him."

"We did, but we're holding him for the time being."

"Why are you so interested in who his aunt's dating?" Alan asked.

"Whoever he is could be close enough to the family to gain access to Rush's phone." Maybe someone did set David Rush up. "If his aunt knows how to get into it." Jake turned his attention to Mac once more. "Anything else you noticed about the guy in the café?"

"He was wearing an earbud." Mac shrugged. "Sam says I should get a pair."

"What about the green panel van?"

"We saw it on the way over and again when it hit Tim."

"And when it pulled in front of us after we left the salvage yard." Sam shuddered.

"Did you get a look at the driver?"

"Tinted glass." Mac shook her head. "That should be illegal."

"I'll bring it up at my next meeting with the governor." Jake smirked.

"Ha ha."

Jake's cellphone buzzed against the table. "Sanders."

"Your prisoner wasn't in a helpful mood. Until I told him the information could help free his sorry soul."

"Who's the lucky man?"

"The lucky *men*. Hank Young and Charles Amory. And, she has his password."

CHAPTER 32

J ake raked his fingers through his hair. He hadn't expected
two names. Especially those two. "Did you know about
your uncle dating Rush's aunt?"

"No." Vic glared at him. "Don't you think I would have
said?"

"Yeah. Sorry." Jake raised a hand in his partner's direction.
"I hoped we were closer to solving this one."

"I know the guy I saw wasn't Hank Young, so it was
probably Charles Amory." Mac leaned forward on the table.
"Do you have a picture of him?"

Vic pulled up a photo on his phone and passed it to Mac.

"I can't say for sure, but from the way he acted with her, it
had to be him."

"But Charles Amory ..." Jake stopped as he realized what he
was about to say. Charles Amory had been the one to identify a
man on a black bicycle with saddlebags. A man with long hair
and red shoes. "Did we ever get a warrant to search the aunt's
house?"

"The guys are there now. We should be getting results soon."

"Who is Charles Amory, if I might ask?" Miss P asked.

"He witnessed a man on a bicycle leaving the scene of the murder." Jake rubbed the back of his neck. "Supposedly. It was his information that led us to suspect David Rush."

"I see." She pushed to her feet. "I believe I will be of better service at the office where I can research this Charles Amory. I will relay any information to you as soon as possible, Detective."

The men stood.

"Thank you, Miss P." Not for the first time, Jake considered hiring the older woman. But he knew his sister and his girlfriend would never speak to him again. Besides, she'd never leave them.

"And I have an evening client." Alan leaned down and planted a kiss on Sam's cheek. "See you later."

She took hold of his hand. "Thanks for being here. I love you."

"Love you more."

A pang of happiness and jealousy shot through Jake. Happiness for his sister and brother-in-law, and jealousy that he didn't have that kind of relationship in his life—yet. He pushed those feelings aside and took his seat. Back to work.

"Do we know of a connection between Amory and Freddy?" Mac made a note on her pad.

"No. He's new to the area. He didn't know anyone before he came here." Jake leaned back in his chair. "Although ... he was a police officer in New York, and Rush did time in New York."

"But what about Freddy? He was in St. Louis." Mac gazed at the far wall. "I wonder if Tim is able to have visitors?"

"He's pretty bad, but I'll check." Jake picked up his phone. It rang in his hand before he could touch a number. "Sanders."

"We finished the search you requested. I'm sending you the results."

"Anything stand out to you?"

"We found the bike right where you said it would be. One of the tires was flat."

"Did it look like it had been ridden lately?"

"Hard to tell. It's pretty dirty. I had it sent back to the lab."

"Anything else?"

"We discovered the pants with the red stripe. Oh, and the red shoes stuffed in a box in the garage."

"Good work. I'll read the rest in your report." The evidence against Rush continued to stack up nice and neat. But was it too convenient? Something nagged at the sixth sense he'd honed since becoming a police officer and wouldn't let him rest.

"Who was that?" Vic asked.

"They've finished the search at Rush's aunt's house. We should be getting a report." Jake stared at his phone and tried to remember what he was about to do before the call.

"I contacted the hospital while you were busy." Mac stood and shrugged into her heavy coat. "Tim can have a visitor or two for a brief period. Will you take me?"

He grunted his assent and got to his feet. "Vic, take Sam home and stay with her until I can arrange a protection detail for her."

"Be glad to."

MAC SETTLED herself in Jake's SUV and studied his profile. "What did they find when they searched the aunt's house, or can't you tell me?"

He cut his eyes over to her. "A black mountain bike, pants with a red stripe, and red shoes."

"All those things back up Charles Amory's witness statement. The question is who's telling the truth?"

"Bingo. He could have used all those details to build a case against David Rush and take any suspicion away from himself."

"Did you ask Rush if he knew Amory before moving to Washington?"

"Not yet. I had no reason to before." Jake tapped the steering wheel. "And Rush had no reason to offer it. When we get to the hospital, I'll call Walker, and he can have another chat with Mr. Rush."

"I feel like we're close to solving this." The anticipation filled her with excitement.

"Even if it turns out to be Hank Young?"

"Sure. Why not?"

"Because you're working for him. Remember?"

She hadn't. The thought pulled her back to reality. If Hank Young was Mr. Big, chances were she wouldn't get paid— again. Why did this keep happening to her? Of course, it could be Charles Amory. Was it okay to pray for someone to be a bad guy? She didn't think so.

"The important thing is we find out who killed Freddy and tried to kill Tim. Along with all the other crimes he's committed." Jake pulled into a parking space at the hospital. "Ready?"

"Yes." She climbed out of the SUV and led the way through the main doors. They took the elevator up and headed for Freddy's room. A police officer, two nurses, and a doctor stood in the hallway arguing.

"What's the problem?" Jake flashed his credentials.

"This man"—The doctor pointed to the officer—"allowed

an unknown doctor to attend to my patient, and now, he's dead."

"Freddy Koenig is dead?" Mac pushed into the circle. She prayed she'd heard him wrong.

"Yes." The doctor glared at her.

"But I talked to a nurse half an hour ago——"

"That was me." A dark-haired woman in scrubs raised her hand. "I'm sorry. We hadn't done our hourly check, and as far as I knew, he was stable and able to have visitors."

The doctor slashed his arms through the air. "What does that matter now? The man is dead all because this idiot let some other idiot into his room."

"Please, calm down, doctor." Jake turned to the officer. "Let's step over here. I need a description of the other doctor." He motioned for Mac to join them.

"He was hunched over so hard to tell his height. Short to medium I'd guess. I couldn't see much else because he looked like he'd just come from the operating room. You know." The officer gestured around his head. "With one of those paper caps on his head and a mask hanging off his ears, and a white coat over blue scrubs." He pointed down. "And those paper booties."

"Was he wearing glasses?" Mac asked.

The man puckered his face in concentration. "Yes. Small ones."

"Was he carrying anything?"

He shook his head. "He had his hands in his pockets."

"Good job. Don't worry, you're not in any trouble," Jake closed his notepad. "You had no way of knowing."

"Thanks, Detective Sanders, but I feel like a fool, and now the guy's dead because of me." He rubbed his forehead. "I don't know how I'll ever get past that."

"We're police officers. We're forced to make choices. Most

of them turn out good, but there's always the one that's not so good. We learn from it and move on." He patted the officer on the back. "You do your best. That's what counts."

The doctor had left by the time Jake and Mac returned to Freddy's room. He waved a nurse over. "How did Mr. Koenig die?"

"From what I understand, the fake doctor gave him a shot of something that stopped his heart."

"Did you see this other doctor?"

"No, none of us did. We were all dealing with other patients."

"Where can we get footage from the hallways?" Mac pointed to the cameras at the ceiling.

"I guess the security office on the first floor." She let out a big sigh. "It's terrible. Just terrible. Is there anything else I can help you with?"

Mac stepped back and surveyed the hallway. "How many patients are on this floor?"

"Five. But they're all at the other end of the hallway. On purpose."

"So, there'd be no reason for anyone to be down here except ...?

"Nurses, his doctor, your police officer, and other hospital staff." She pinched her lips together in thought. "And the cleaning staff."

"Thanks. You've been a big help." Jake shook her hand and led Mac to the elevators.

On the first floor, he got directions to the security office. Jake knocked and showed his credentials to the guard inside.

"What do you want to see?" The man in the gray uniform punched a button, and a tray slid out.

"We're most interested in the cameras on the second-floor hallway around room ten within the last two hours."

"Oh. That should be on what we're recording now. Let me make a copy, and we can look at it. It should only take a few minutes."

"Where's the lady's room?" Mac went to the door.

"Across the hall on your right." The guard waved a hand in the general direction. "Knock when you get back."

"Thanks." Mac hurried over to the door marked Women.

Two regular stalls and one for handicapped were tucked along the left side with two sinks on the right. One of the stalls opened as she entered, and she ducked inside. Voices from two women echoed off the beige tiled walls and floor. Followed by the rush of water, the roar of hand dryers, and the bang of the door to the hall.

Quiet descended on the room. Mac was tempted to stay in the closed-in gray metal space a little longer. Until she felt the pressure change as the door opened—without a sound. She stood, pulling her pants up as quietly as possible.

The click of a lock. Every nerve in her body went on high alert. Someone was in the restroom with her, and they'd locked the door to the hallway.

CHAPTER 33

Mac peered out from the stall as best she could. No one in sight.

The lights went out.

Her muscles tensed. She would fight with every ounce of her strength.

"Miss Love. I know you're in here."

She willed her ears to pick up any familiar intonations in the voice. None. Too raspy.

"All I care about is the coin. Give it to me, and I promise to get out of your life forever."

"I don't have it." Mac struggled to keep her own voice from shaking.

"But you know where it is. Get it."

"How can I contact you?"

The lock sounded again, and a breath of air swirled around her ankles. Had he left? Or was he waiting for her to come out of the stall?

"Mac." A bang on the door. "Are you okay?"

"Jake. Open the door but be careful." The lights came on. No sounds of a scuffle.

"What happened? Why are you in the dark?"

She burst out of the stall and pushed past him into the hallway. "Did you see anyone out here?"

"No. Why?"

"I had a visit in the restroom from Mr. Big." She dropped into a chair against the wall.

"What did he look like?" Jake yanked his phone from his pocket. "I'll lock down the hospital and start a manhunt."

"I didn't get a look at him." She propped her head in her hands. "I was in a stall, and he turned the lights out."

"How do you know it was him?"

"He called me by name and said all he wants is the coin." She clenched her fists at the memory of his words. "When I said I didn't have it, he told me to get it and get in touch with him."

"How are you supposed to do that?"

"Good question." But somehow, she knew it wouldn't be a problem. She lifted her eyes to Jake and the guard. "Did you find anything on the security tape?"

"Only what the officer described. A doctor in scrubs and a white coat with a cap and a mask."

"I guess I'd better check the cameras in this hallway now." The guard returned to the security room.

"Thanks." Jake pulled a chair next to Mac. "Are you okay?" He reached for her hand.

She slipped her hand in his and nodded. There was a point in the dark when the nightmares from last year threatened to return, but she managed to hold them at bay. She leaned her head on his shoulder. "I'm fine. Just tired."

The guard popped his head out the door from the security room. "You're going to want to see this."

Mac and Jake squinted over the guard's shoulder at the screen. They saw Mac enter the restroom. A few minutes later, two women left in animated conversation, and headed to the right, down the hall.

A moment later, a figure in blue scrubs, a white lab coat, and with a cap over his head came into view from their left. He pulled the door open with a gloved hand.

"He's got his back to us. I can't make out his face," Jake said. "Have you got any other views?"

"The guy knows where the cameras are. He came from the stairwell around the corner where he stood with the door cracked, but he kept his head down and face covered the whole way."

"Where did he go when he left the restroom?"

The guard sped through the frames on the monitor until the man in the white lab coat slipped through the door marked Women. He checked both directions before hurrying off screen to their left. "He took the stairs to the first floor and headed out a side door."

"Any cameras in the parking lot?"

"Yes, but there are blind spots and shadows after dark. This guy must know where they are because he disappears. Unless he's really good at disguises."

A view of the side parking lot came up on the monitor. Two children dashed between the parked cars to a van followed by a mom carrying an infant. An old man made his way slowly across the lot hunched over a walker. He stopped next to a large four-door sedan. A woman in a hooded fur parka and skinny jeans sashayed over to a low red car.

"Stop." Mac leaned in closer. "Is that David's aunt?"

"Hard to tell in the low light with her back to us." Jake made a note of the car. "I'll check with the DMV. Tell me about the blind spots."

"The cameras are pointed at the lot, not at the door. Anyone could step out the door, stay back against the building, and not be detected."

"But how could he get to his car?"

"If he angled straight out at the corner, I don't think either camera would pick him up." The guard shrugged. "Or he could change clothes and walk out to his car."

"He'd be taking a risk of someone coming out and seeing him changing. Wouldn't he?"

"There're some tall shrubs he could hide behind."

Jake opened the door. "Let's check. Can you see your monitor on your phone?"

"Yes." The guard pulled the door shut behind him and punched some buttons on his phone. "I'm ready."

Mac zipped her jacket and hitched her purse onto her shoulder as they climbed the stairs to the first floor.

"You stay here and watch your monitor while Mac and I go out along the walls of the building on either side of the door." Jake looked at her. "Okay with you?"

She nodded. It felt good to be doing something constructive. "I'll go right."

Jake let her go first. She hugged herself against the biting wind and pulled her hat down farther on her head. Two steps out, she turned right.

A low wall blocked her from staying next to the building. She turned on her flashlight, swung her leg over the wall, and studied the ground on the other side. The niche formed by the building and the wall had been protected from the brunt of the bad weather. No footprints would show on the dry leaves covering the dirt.

She hopped down and continued along the wall of the building, watching for any signs another person had passed through there recently. When she got to a large fir tree, she stopped. She couldn't imagine anyone pushing his way in amongst those scratchy branches to change clothes.

But she was there to investigate. She closed her eyes, drew her arms up against her chest, and pressed against the branches. They gave, and when they sprang back behind her, she found herself in a dark cavity. Someone had cut the branches away from the trunk and made this hideaway. She shone her light around.

And there at her feet lay a bulging backpack. Mac couldn't wait to tell Jake. She hoisted the pack and turned to leave. A figure with a helmet over his head and dressed all in black pushed into the small space from the other side. He shoved her to the ground, the beam of her flashlight dancing wildly about, and yanked the backpack from her hand. As quickly as he appeared, he was gone.

Mac roared in rage and frustration. She leaped to her feet and pressed through the dense bush after her attacker. The deep rumble of a powerful motorcycle engine reached her as she rounded the corner. Too late.

Jake and the guard rushed up next to her.

"What happened?"

"I found the place where our perp changed his clothes, and I even found the clothes, but—" She gestured into the distance. "He came back for them and caught me by surprise."

"You let him get away?"

She glared at Jake. "He had a big motorcycle. What was I supposed to do?"

He raised a hand to her cheek. "You're beautiful face. I'm sorry, Mac."

The salt from his hand stung the scratches on her skin, but she tried not to wince.

"We'll get him. The motorcycle must be on camera." Jake glanced at the guard. "Right?"

"Yep. We got him now."

But after they pulled up the security camera footage, Mac and Jake stared at the screen in amazement. This guy was good. He managed to get through the parking lot without giving them any good shots of him or his motorcycle.

"This isn't the only place with cameras." Jake stood. "Come on, Mac. We're going hunting."

She glanced at the monitor again. Considering the man's skill so far, she gave them a so-so chance of success.

CHAPTER 34

J ake stopped. The scratches on Mac's face had turned to angry red welts. "But we're not going anywhere until you see a doctor." He escorted her through the door and toward the emergency room.

"I'm fine." She whirled away from him. "I'll put a little anti-itch cream on them and drink plenty of water."

"What was it you said to Miss P about getting looked at?" Jake glared at her. "That it's good business to look after your employees?"

"I'm not an employee. I'm a boss."

"That's for sure." He stood face to face with her, arms locked across his chest. "And I'm the police."

"Are you ordering me to see the doctor?" She stepped closer, her chestnut eyes flashing at him.

He relaxed his stance with a smile. "It was worth a try."

"Well. Maybe I should. We're here." She touched her face and grimaced. "It does hurt a little. And itch."

"When you're done, we'll go to the station." He led the way

to Emergency, and after getting her admitted, he settled into a chair to wait.

Out of habit, Jake chose a spot where he could view the entire waiting room. His eyes tracked all the comings and goings while his mind evaluated Charles Amory as a suspect. How could Amory be the man behind the theft and the killings? The man was new to the area. He didn't know anyone, or almost no one.

Yet he supposedly got Freddy Koenig to break into the time capsule and Owen Baker, the Chief's brother, to keep tabs on Mackenzie. And, he was dating David Rush's aunt, Katherine Underwood—which is probably where he heard of the mule half dollar in the first place. Time to bring Mr. Amory in for a talk.

"There you are." Mac wove her way across the room to him.

"What's the verdict?" He rose. "Will you live?"

"Anti-itch cream." She peered at him and then gave him a sheepish smile. "Plus, an antibiotic. It seems fir branches can carry mold and other nasty things on them that get under your skin."

"Good thing you saw the doc." He kept his face neutral.

"Yep." She dug in her purse for her phone. "Mackenzie Love." Her face darkened as she listened intently. "Mr. Young, whoever told you I had the coin, lied to you." She glanced at Jake. "Yes, the police have recovered the rest of the items from the time capsule, and you may come to the station to see them. But they're evidence. You can't take them yet."

Frustration creased her brow and pinched her lips together. Jake motioned to her to hand him the phone. "Mr. Young, this is Detective Sanders. Miss Love and I worked together to retrieve your items. Meet us at the police station, and we'll continue this discussion."

"Yes, of course, Detective Sanders. I didn't realize—"

"Ten minutes." Jake pushed End before he said something he'd regret. "I hate bullies."

After a few minutes of silence, Mac cleared her throat. "I could have handled him."

"I know. Thanks for letting me be the one." He reached for her hand.

"You're welcome." She slipped her hand into his and squeezed.

Which he knew meant thank you.

The SUV bounced into the station house parking lot, and Jake steered it into his usual spot. "Do we tell Young about the coin?"

"I don't know." Mac slid to the ground and shut the door. "I wonder how he knew we found it?"

"Me too." Jake followed her into the building. "Let's see if we can find out where he heard it from first before we say anything."

She nodded.

In his office, he picked up the receiver on his desk phone. "Walters, I need any surveillance cameras at businesses or homes around the hospital checked for a motorcycle about one hour ago."

"On it."

Mac puffed her cheeks out and blew out a couple of times.

"How are you feeling?"

"Not bad. They're beginning to sting." She hovered her hands over the scratches on her cheeks for a second. "I think I'll go put some more cream on them."

"Before you go, what was Young saying to you before you handed the phone to me?"

"It's nothing." She stiffened with her hand on the doorknob.

"I could tell it was not nothing, Mac."

"He said since the police found the items from the time capsule, he was inclined not to pay us."

Anger churned in his chest. "We'll see about that."

"No, Jake." She moved in front of his desk and leaned on it. "This one has to be my battle."

Her beautiful chestnut eyes shone with intensity, and, as hard as it would be, he needed to do what she asked. "Okay."

"Thank you." She turned and left the room.

He picked up the phone once more. "Vic, your uncle is coming into the station, and I think you should be here."

"On my way."

Detective Victor Young and Mac got to the office just in time. Two minutes later, there was a rap on the door, and Hank Young entered.

"Thanks for coming, Mr. Young," Jake said. "I understand you think Miss Love has possession of a certain coin?"

"You get right to the point."

"Answer the question, please."

"I heard it from a reliable source." The older man threw Jake a piercing look.

But he'd dealt with men like him before and assumed the stone face he used in these situations. "What reliable source?"

"I'd rather not say." His demeanor changed, and the man squirmed in his chair. "Especially if it's not true."

"We'd rather you did. In fact, I'm insisting you do." Jake continued to stare at the man across from him. "The information could lead us to a thief and a killer."

Hank Young raised a hand to his now pale forehead. "I hardly think the person—"

"Let me be the judge of that."

"Katherine. Katherine Underwood." He turned pleading eyes on first Jake and then his nephew, Vic. "But I can't imagine she could be involved in anything like this."

"Did she ask you to contact Mac? To see if she really did have the coin?"

"Yes." His voice dropped to a whisper.

"I'm sorry. What did you say?"

He straightened. "Yes."

"Mr. Young, I want you to think very carefully about my next question." Anticipation sparked through him. Even the air seemed to be holding its breath. "Were you involved in any way with the theft of the items from the time capsule and the subsequent murders of Freddy Koenig and Owen Baker?"

"No!" Young leaped to his feet, his face contorted with horror. "I'd never ... I couldn't."

Vic put his hands on his uncle's shoulders and eased him down into his chair. "Sit down, Hank."

Jake focused on his notes for a moment until the tension in the room subsided. His intuition told him Hank Young was telling the truth. If so, he could be of use to them.

CHAPTER 35

"Y ou can go, Mr. Young." Jake raised his gaze to the man across from him.

Hank Young squared his shoulders. "Detective, I came here to view the contents of the time capsule."

"Oh, yes. Detective Young will take you to see them." As the man rose, Jake raised a hand. "Mr. Young, I believe you. We do have the coin." Jake tapped his pocket.

"May I see it?"

Jake extracted the clear bag containing the half dollar and held it out to him. "Hard to believe something so small has led to such destruction and loss of life." He held out his hand.

Young placed the bag in his palm and shook his head. "I don't understand it either, Detective."

Vic escorted his uncle to the door.

"One more question. Where were you today from about three to six this afternoon?"

"I was in a meeting with the mayor and two other gentlemen. We ended up having an early dinner together."

Jake made a note and nodded in his direction. "That's all

for now." An alibi he could check, and if it was true, Hank Young had nothing to do with Tim Koenig's death. Which would support his theory that Young wasn't involved.

"Why did you do that?" Mac scowled at him. "I thought you didn't want me to tell anyone. Especially Hank Young."

"I'm baiting the hook." Jake stared at the closed door.

"You mean you set yourself up as bait."

He shrugged and yawned.

"Don't do that." Mac groaned. "You'll get me started."

"Come on." He rose. "I should have sent you home earlier." Dark circles rimmed her eyes over swollen cheeks.

"I wanted to hear what Young had to say." She started to stand but plopped down in the chair again. "I'm dizzy. Do you think that's the meds?"

"You haven't had anything to eat since lunch." Jake placed an arm around her waist and helped her up. "We'll grab a burger on our way back. I don't want you driving like this. We can get your car tomorrow."

"Fine with me."

Burger, fries, and an iced tea—her go-to meal. She scarfed the food down between the restaurant and home and felt better already. Normally, she didn't like eating right before going to bed, but tonight she'd made an exception. Jake's SUV was warm and cozy, and with a full stomach, she found it hard to keep her eyes open.

"Wake up, sleepy head. We're home."

His soft voice brought a smile to her face. Wouldn't it be wonderful if home meant the same place to both of them? The ring of his phone jarred her awake.

"Calm down, Sam."

Every nerve in her body sparked at the name of her best friend.

Jake pressed speaker, and Sam's terrified whisper came through loud and clear.

"Someone's in the house. I'm in the master bath upstairs."

"Alan's not there?"

"No."

"Could it be him coming home?"

"No."

"Where's Killer?"

"In the bedroom."

"I'm handing the phone to Mac so I can call for help."

"Sam, it's me." She strove for a calm tone of voice.

"I'm scared."

"I know. Listen, what do you have that could be used as a weapon?"

"In my bathroom?" The quiet opening and closing of drawers and doors came over the speakers. "Toilet cleaner's the best I can do."

"Great. You can spray it in his eyes." It probably wouldn't be enough to save her, but at least Sam would feel as if she had some control. "We're on our way, and Jake called it in. You probably won't need it."

"I hope not." Killer's frenzied barking ratcheted up a notch. "Mac, I ..."

A crash followed by a canine yelp of pain left Mac paralyzed with fear. What was happening? The sound of splintering wood, closer this time, and a shriek that set her teeth on edge. "Sam. Sam." Mac cried her friend's name into the phone as noises of a struggle echoed through the car.

"We're two blocks away," Jake yelled to her.

A dreadful silence settled over the car that was more

terrible than anything that had gone before. A scream clawed at Mac's throat.

"Sam? Are you there?" Jake yelled his question into the void.

Nothing.

A squad car barreled into Sam's driveway ahead of Jake's SUV. Police tumbled out and ran for the door.

"Wait. I have a key," Jake said.

But the door stood open. Tears streamed down Mac's face. She made no attempt to brush them away. If anything had happened to her friend or the baby, she wasn't sure how she could ever live with herself. She followed Jake into the house.

"Be careful not to touch anything."

They took the steps with care and hugged the wall until they came to the master bedroom. Killer lay on his side inside the busted door, his eyes closed. A stab of pain shot through Mac's chest.

"Sam."

The echo of Jake's voice came to her from the master bath, and she rushed across the room. Her sweet friend lay, eyes shut, sprawled on the bathroom floor, the can of cleaner near her right hand. "Is she?"

"She's got a pulse." Jake called for an ambulance. "Let's back out of here. I need to take some pictures."

All Mac wanted was to hold her best friend's head in her lap, but she knew the only way to catch who did this was to gather evidence. Some of which they'd already trampled on their way upstairs.

"Jake." Alan's urgent cry reached them from below. "Where's Sam? Is she all right?"

"I'll go." Mac retraced their steps to the front door and led Alan away from the house. "She's breathing. An ambulance is on its way."

"Oh no." He sank to the gravel driveway. "I wanted to cancel this client, but she insisted. And we needed some things from the grocery ..." He put his head in his hands. "If anything happens to her or the baby, I'll never forgive myself."

Mac dropped down beside him. His words were like a punch to her stomach. "It's not your fault. It's mine. If I hadn't asked her to be my partner, no one would be after her in the first place."

"No." Alan glared at her. "Don't ever say that. Samantha loves her work with you. She sees it as her mission. She and I have come to grips with the fact it will be dangerous at times. So don't you ever try to take that away from her."

"But what about the baby? Doesn't that change things for you two?"

"We've talked about it, and Sam wants to continue working. She may have to cut the hours she's in the office, but she can work from home, can't she?"

"Sure."

"And I plan on arranging my schedule so I'm available to be home to do daddy care for her as well."

"Her?" Mac gave him a sharp look. "You're having a girl?"

"Don't tell her I said anything." Alan scrunched up his face. "She wants to tell you herself."

A spark of joy pushed aside the darkness and allowed hope to flow into her soul. She gave Alan a hug. "Don't worry about Sam. She's a fighter."

An ambulance screamed down the street, and they jumped to their feet. The emergency crew raced into the house. Mac paced the walkway. What was taking so long? They needed to get Sam to the hospital as soon as possible. Finally, she heard the wheels of the gurney and the men chatting with a woman. A woman?

As the gurney passed her, Sam looked up. "Thanks for the advice about the spray cleaner. It saved my life."

Mac's mouth gaped open.

"Close your mouth, dear, it's very unbecoming." The words trailed away as the EMTs loaded Sam into the ambulance.

Jake came up beside her. "They gave her a shot of something. It won't harm the baby."

"I could tell. Whatever it was, I'm just thankful she's alive."

"Me too."

Jake wrapped his arm around her, and she realized for the first time she was cold and very, very tired.

Shouting from behind peaked her adrenaline once more. Killer streaked out of the house and leaped into the ambulance with teeth bared and hair on end. The EMTs scrambled out a side door. He leaned on the gurney next to Sam, quivering. She'd forgotten about the dog after seeing her friend on the bathroom floor. Now, a second wave of relief flowed through her.

Alan approached with slow steps and hands outstretched. "Hey, big boy. It's me, buddy."

The dog gave a menacing growl.

Sam murmured something to him, and he sniffed the air. His tail gave a tentative wag. Alan stroked his head, and he yelped. After several moments, Alan slipped a hand through his collar and coaxed him out of the ambulance.

"He's been hit on the head. Hard." Alan pinned Jake's eyes with a look of intense anger. "Get this ..."

"I will."

"I need to go with Sam, but Killer needs to go to the emergency vet clinic. Can you take him?"

"I'll send him with Vic."

Alan shook his head. "He's too traumatized. I don't think he'll go with someone he doesn't know."

"Let Vic take me home, and you look after Killer." Mac touched Jake's arm. "I'll be fine."

"I don't want you staying alone." He gave her a stern look. "Vic will stay with you until Miss P or somebody can come. I'll check on you later."

She nodded and pressed Call on her phone. "Miss P? I have a favor to ask."

"Whatever you need, my dear."

Her friend's words brought a smile to her face. "Could you come stay with me tonight?"

"I'd be glad to. I can be there in half an hour. Would that suit?"

"Perfect."

"By the way, I think you should know my nephew, Nathanial, is being released on probation. He has petitioned to come live with me if I agree."

"So soon?" A lump formed in her throat, and she found it hard to swallow.

"It seems he was able to provide the prosecutor with needed information and, therefore, able to reduce his sentence."

Mac grabbed Jake's sleeve before he left. "What have you decided?"

"I haven't yet, but I found it interesting that if I do, he told me his probation officer will be Charles Amory."

CHAPTER 36

Mac and Miss P agreed not to discuss Nate. She needed sleep. But her sheets told the tale of a less than peaceful night—one filled with dreams bordering on nightmares about her kidnapping and betrayal by her former boyfriend who knew about it and let it happen.

Washington was a small town. How could she do life in the same town with him? And what about Miss P? She was his only living relative, and a beloved friend and employee to her. What would happen to their relationship?

She opened her curtains on another gray January day. No help there. With a sigh, she settled into her armchair and read her daily meditation and Bible readings. "Seek God's perspective and realize all is in His Will. He's in control no matter what." She gazed out the window. "I understand, but I need Your help remembering this when things get messy."

Time to put thoughts of Nate aside. She had other concerns to deal with. Like finding out who attacked Sam. She yanked a brush through her hair and pulled it into a ponytail. One piece of information that might help. She now knew Charles Amory was a probation officer.

"Mackenzie, my dear." Miss P cracked the door to her room. "Jake is meeting us at Samantha's home in twenty minutes. I have coffee and a roll prepared for you to eat on the way."

"I'm ready." She headed down the hall after her former chemistry teacher, slipped into her coat, and locked the door behind her. Her mouth watered as she entered Miss P's car. "Where did you get the pastries?"

"I brought them from the office. With your busy schedule, I assumed there wouldn't be adequate food in the house."

Ouch. "Thank you. You know me well."

"My pleasure. I enjoy taking care of you and Samantha."

Mac washed down a bite of lemon cream with a swig of hot coffee. "I need to say something to you about Nate."

"My dear, I understand, and your well-being will be a major consideration in making my decision. You're—"

"No, please. I wanted to say I'm okay with Nate coming back to Washington. You're his only living relative, and he needs you."

Miss P stopped at an intersection and turned to face Mac. "After what he did to you, I'm not sure I can forgive him. This will be a difficult decision for me. I know I should, but it will require a lot of prayer."

Tears welled in Mac's eyes. She thanked God for Miss P. There had been a hole in her heart ever since she'd lost her parents, and she cherished the nurturing love this amazing woman gave her. She ached to share the truth about her family with the older woman, and to get her wise counsel about the inheritance, but she couldn't. Not without her sisters' permission.

"I love you, Miss P." She gulped back the tears in her throat.

"I love you as well, my dear." She smiled. "You've given me something I never thought I'd have. I feel as if I have been granted a daughter." She patted Mac's arm. "Now, Detective Sanders and the others will be wondering where we are."

"Speaking of which, I thought Sam's house would still be considered a crime scene." Mac swiped at her cheeks with a tissue.

"I take it he was able to speed things along so Samantha could return to her home from the hospital."

"She's home?" Sunlight broke through the clouds and warmed her heart. "The baby's okay?"

"As far as I know."

"And Killer?"

"He sustained quite a blow to the head and requires further intravenous fluids and rest, poor pup. The veterinarian thought it best to keep him at the hospital for observation another day."

Sam's front door opened before they turned into the drive, and Jake jogged over to the car. "Good to see you. Any trouble last night?"

"No." Mac's skin prickled as she followed his gaze down the street the way they'd come. "What's wrong?"

"Time to talk when we're inside." He placed one hand on her back and the other on Miss P's elbow and hurried them up the walk and through the front door. "We're in the back."

Samantha smiled at her from the recliner where she sat feet up and a beautiful patchwork quilt tucked in around her. Mac crossed the room in three strides and sat on the couch beside her. "I want to hear it from you."

"I'm fine, and the baby's fine." She placed a hand on Mac's arm.

The last shred of worry wafted away, and she was ready to focus. "Okay. Good." Mac rose. "Any coffee in this place?"

"Coming up." Alan left the room.

"And bring me my computer, hon," Sam called after him.

"Do you think that's wise, Samantha?" Miss P peered at her over the rim of her glasses.

"Probably not, but I promise not to overdo it. On my honor." Sam held up two fingers as if pledging.

"I believe that's the Cub Scout salute. The Girl Scout salute is three fingers."

"Oh." She giggled and added a third finger.

Mac sat at the small breakfast table facing her friend. The idea of brainstorming together filled her with joy, but she'd keep an eye on her partner. Any sign she was tiring, and they'd stop. "Where are we?" She pulled a large pad and pencil from her roomy handbag.

"We can be pretty sure David Rush isn't our killer." Sam placed a pillow on her lap as a makeshift desk for her computer.

"Yes." Jake handed Mac a mug of coffee and sat beside her. "Charles Amory is in this up to his receding hairline. He gave us the witness statements about Rush."

"Unless someone dressed in David's clothes and rode his bike to kill Freddy."

"Who'd have access to his stuff?"

"I can think of only one person." Mac looked up from her notes. "His aunt."

"But what about the hair out the back of the ski mask?"

"Pfft. Easy. A wig."

"She did have first-hand knowledge of the mule coin," Miss P said.

"And she knows all the major players." Alan held up a hand and pointed to fingers as he spoke. "Freddy Koenig, Owen Baker, David, Tim Koenig."

"But would she try to frame her nephew?"

"She hasn't seen him for a long time. Possibly they aren't as close as they once were." Miss P glanced at Mac.

"She did say she wouldn't lend him money for his art studio because she didn't trust him."

"And the doctor in the hospital was bundled up. Hard to tell if it was a man or a woman." Jake turned to Mac. "You thought you saw Rush's aunt on the security footage. Remember?"

"Did you ever check with the DMV about the car?"

"I'll do it now." He picked up his phone. "I'll see if she's got a motorcycle too."

Miss P placed some files on the table and took a chair at one end. "While Detective Sanders is taking care of that, might I show you what I found on Charles Amory?" She opened a folder and passed out papers to everyone. "I believe this could be helpful."

Mac scanned the sheet and began again at the top, reading what was typed word for word. When she finished, she leaned back and found Sam staring at her. All the puzzle pieces they had carefully been constructing just got jumbled, and they were back to square one.

CHAPTER 37

The jangle of Mac's phone jarred the silence. Zoe. She almost didn't answer, but ... "Hi."

"You did it to me again." The woman's bruised feelings traveled through the speaker. "You told me I was part of the team, but now you've disappeared altogether."

"I'm so sorry, Zoe. We're at Sam's. She was attacked last night."

"Oh gosh."

"I'll text you the address. But first, there's something I need you to do for me. A job."

"What? You're not putting me off, are you?"

"No. This is important. I'm going to text you a photo of Charles Amory. I need you to go by the police station and talk to David. See if he recognizes Amory. Ask him if he knew him in New York. It's important."

"Will they let me in?"

"I'll have Jake call ahead. After you do that, come straight here." Mac hesitated. "Be careful."

"Got it."

"I could have had one of my guys talk to him." Jake gave her an irritated look.

"David trusts her. He's more likely to tell her about any connection in New York than a police officer." Mac scrolled through her photos and sent off the one of Amory. "What did you find out from the DMV?"

"The red sporty car belongs to a woman from Herman." He held up his phone with the woman's driver's license. "She looks a little like Rush's aunt. No joy on the motorcycle. She could have paid someone."

"Or he. You need to read the information Miss P discovered on Charles Amory." Mac tapped the paper in front of him. "When he left the police force, he became a probation officer. In St. Louis."

Jake whistled. "Freddy Koenig was his client."

"Yes." Mac scribbled on her pad. "Here's the question I'm wrestling with—are Charles and Katherine in it together?"

"Two hundred thousand doesn't go as far as it used to. Is there something we're missing here?" Jake sipped his coffee. "Especially when they can't afford to sell it outright. They won't get near that much for it."

"If they had the last one in existence, that would be different." Sam ran a finger down her screen. "But there's still another one out there somewhere."

"What if they have that one already?" Alan asked.

"As in own it?"

He shrugged. "Or stole it."

Silence descended on the room as each one of them worked out the possible value to an unscrupulous collector. Until Mac remembered one crucial detail. There was one more coin in existence. She pressed her pencil on her pad until the point broke with a crack.

While she rummaged in her bag for another one, her mind

wrestled with whether to betray her promise to Mrs. White. What if whoever was behind this knew about the coin at the museum? Mac would never forgive herself if something happened to anyone there. Especially her friend.

She scanned the faces in the room. All people she trusted and knew Mrs. White could trust as well. "There is one more mule coin. It's at the historical museum."

"How do you know?"

"Mrs. White showed it to me. She swore me to secrecy because she's concerned someone might try to steal it." Mac sighed. "Under the circumstances, I think her fears are justified."

"Who knows about it?"

"According to her, the woman in charge of the memorabilia and the people at the museum at that time."

"Is there any chance Katherine Underwood would know? She was the head teller at the bank, and in charge of giving out and retrieving the coins." Sam stretched and flexed her fingers.

"I wouldn't doubt it. She's got connections all over town."

"She's dating Hank Young, and he was on the sesquicentennial committee." Miss P stood and collected empty mugs.

Alan jumped up. "I can do that."

"Nonsense. I need to feel useful. You take care of Samantha."

Mac's phone rang again, and she pressed Speaker. "Zoe, what did David say?"

"He's not there. He's been released."

"Who released him?" Jake slapped the table.

"How should I know?"

"Sorry." Jake ran a hand through his hair. "Are you still at the precinct?"

"Yes."

"Go to the receptionist and put your phone on speaker."

"Detective Sanders wants to speak to you."

"Excuse me?" An irritated female voice echoed in the room.

"This is Detective Jake Sanders. I need to know who okayed the release of David Rush."

"Detective Sanders or whoever you are. I can't give you that information. You'll have to call back on a secure phone."

Mac cringed inside. *Or whoever you are?*

"Did you hear her?" Zoe asked.

Jake strode to the front door and out onto the porch.

"He heard it. Come over to Sam's."

"No. I'm going to find David. I'll keep you informed."

"Be careful," Mac said before she realized she was talking to air.

Jake blew in on a blast of frigid air. "The Chief let Rush go. Orders from above. I'm meeting Vic at Katherine Underwood's place for another interview. I'll let you know what I find out."

Mac pushed to her feet and rushed to catch him. "I want to come."

"Not this time." He cradled her face in his hands.

"I'll stay in the background."

"She responds better to men." He kissed her. "You understand."

She did, but she didn't like it. "Where's the mule coin?"

"Safe." He tapped his breast pocket. "I have to go."

A sudden foreboding slid through her veins like cold needles. She ran outside, but it was too late. He was gone.

CHAPTER 38

The door was opened by a woman with dull gray hair and bags under her eyes. Gone was the make-up and gold jewelry. This was the raw Katherine Underwood.

"Go away. I can't talk right now." She braced the door half way closed.

"We're not going away. Either we talk here, or we talk at the station."

She flung the door open and turned her back on them. The men followed her up the stairs to the living area. At the kitchen, she staggered and reached for the island for support.

Jake stepped over to her. "Are you all right?"

She dissolved into tears and flung herself against him. "The most terrible thing has happened, and I don't know what to do."

"Why don't we sit down, and you can tell us about it?" Jake patted her back and tried to step away from her embrace.

She moved her hands under his jacket and clung to him. "Please. I need to feel the warmth of another human being for a moment."

"I understand, but—" Compassion for the older woman warred with his training as a police officer. Such a fine line to walk.

With swift movements, she unsnapped his holster and withdrew his gun. She backed away and pointed it at him. "Stay where you are, or I will shoot."

Jake motioned for Vic to do as she said. "I guess you answered our questions, Miss Underwood."

"What questions were those?"

"About the theft and murders. You're involved. Along with your boyfriend, Charles Amory."

"He's not my boyfriend." She spat the words at them. "He's the devil incarnate."

"Then I don't get it. Why this?" Jake inclined his head toward her.

"Because he has David and is demanding the mule coin, or he'll kill him." A tear slid down her cheek. "Give it to me."

"I don't have it." He held her gaze and inched a step closer.

"Don't try me, Detective. I've never killed anyone before, but I will kill you and your partner to get the coin and save David."

The smell of desperation pervaded the room, and he knew she meant what she said. "Okay. But tell me how you got mixed up in this." He made a show of fishing in his breast pocket for the coin.

"Amory came to me. He'd secured one of the coins and wanted all of them. He knew David was my ... nephew, and he knew David had been in prison for forgery." Her gaze remained focused on Jake. "Yes, I knew. David, God love him, thinks he's kept it a secret from me."

Her hands trembled a little. It was a heavy gun. There was a chance he could defuse the situation if only Vic didn't try anything stupid.

"Lay the coin on the counter."

"He threatened to mess things up for David if you didn't help him." He placed the half-dollar where she indicated.

"My, my. Figured that out all by yourself, did you?"

"I also figured out David's more than just a nephew to you." Jake studied her face.

"How do you ...?" She blanched. "No one knows."

"I didn't. Until now."

"My sister couldn't have children. They asked me to carry a child for them. When they were killed, I ended up bringing David up as my nephew, but he's really my son." Her face softened at the word, but hardened again as she picked up the coin. "I'd do anything to save him."

"We can help you." Jake took a step toward her. "We know how to—"

"Don't come any closer." Her voice rose, and her hands tightened around the pistol.

Vic moved around Jake and hurried in her direction, gun drawn.

"No." Jake flung his arm out to stop him.

She swiveled Jake's gun in Vic's direction and pulled the trigger. He collapsed to the floor. Jake knelt by his friend.

A look of horror distorted her face.

"Katherine, call for help." Jake spoke with authority and prayed she would respond automatically.

At first, it seemed as if she would, but she looked at the gun in her hand, and her face took on a new look, one of resolution. She threw the pistol across the room, tossed a kitchen towel in his direction, and raced for the back door.

"I'm sorry."

The words reached him as a choked cry as she disappeared. The sound of a motorcycle reverberated off the building, and a wave of cold air streamed through the open door. Jake pressed the cloth on Vic's wound.

"Keep pressure on this for a second. I'll call an ambulance." Jake jumped to his feet, closed the slider, and called for help.

"Good thing she's a bad shot." Vic grimaced. "I think she grazed me, but it sure hurts."

"Stop talking and lay still." Jake retrieved another dishtowel. Lots of blood. Not good. Where was the ambulance?

Familiar sounds came from outside, and paramedics hurried through the sliding glass doors. Jake gave Vic a thumbs up and moved away. He yanked his phone from his pocket and dialed the Chief. "We've got a problem."

"What now?"

"Katherine Underwood has the mule coin, and she's taking it to Charles Amory as ransom for her nephew, David Rush."

"How did that happen?"

"It's a long story. She got my gun and shot Vic. He'll be fine, but he's on his way to the hospital."

"Great. This just keeps getting better and better. I'll send someone to process the scene. You need to get back here so we can figure out what to mess up next."

"Yes, sir." Dread like a ball of lead settled in Jake's stomach. He should have tried to get his gun back right away, but he kept thinking he could talk her out of it. The gurney went by with Vic strapped down and an oxygen mask on his face. "Will he be okay?"

"Should be. He lost some blood, but it looks like it missed anything vital."

"Why the oxygen?"

"We do it as a precaution."

Jake nodded. Guys showed up in paper suits and booties. They snapped pictures and dusted for fingerprints. His heart lurched as they drew a circle around the blood pool where Vic had fallen. His phone rang. Mac. "Bad time. Can't talk right now." He pressed End.

Detective Walker came through the door just as they finished. "The Chief sent me to take your statement and follow you back to the station." He rubbed the bridge of his nose. "Sorry, Jake."

"I understand." He massaged his forehead. As he related the details to Walker, he struggled to keep his anger at bay. How had he let this happen? A skinny little old lady had taken his gun from him. Maybe it was time for him to get out of the field and ride a desk.

"Okay. That should do it for now." Walker threw him a grim smile. "Ready to go?"

Jake nodded. "What about Underwood?"

"We've got an APB out on her and the motorcycle, and Charles Amory."

As they walked out the door, Walker's phone sounded. He answered and glanced at Jake. "We're leaving now." He turned to Jake. "Good. Thanks for letting me know." He pressed End. "They've found Katherine Underwood. They're bringing her in to the station."

CHAPTER 39

A fierce hope buoyed Jake's spirit. He was eager to resume his questioning of Katherine Underwood and redeem himself if not in his Chief's eyes, at least to himself.

"She didn't have the coin." Walker stopped at his car.

"But she'll know where it is." Jake jogged across the street to his SUV and jumped inside. And he intended to find out where she left it.

At the precinct, the Chief waited at the top of the stairs. "In my office." He pivoted on his heel and marched down the corridor.

"I know you're mad, but—"

"Close the door." His boss indicated the chair across from him.

"I need to interview Katherine Underwood." He pointed back the way they'd come.

"Sit." Chief Baker fixed him with a look that left no room for discussion.

Jake sat.

"If it were anyone else, I would be taking his badge and

putting him on probation." The Chief held up his hand to silence any answer from Jake. "You messed up big time. Not only did you lose your weapon to a suspect, but the suspect used it to shoot another officer."

Jake felt the full force of the other man's words.

"Luckily, Vic is okay. I spoke to him on the phone, and he's staying overnight in the hospital, but should be released tomorrow." The Chief leaned back and laced his fingers over his stomach. "I'm not sure what sort of reprimand I'm going to give you, but for now, go home."

"But—"

"Walker is interviewing her. I want you to leave, Jake."

"Chief, we're so close to solving this, and there's something else."

"What?" He let out an exasperated sigh.

"We believe Amory will try for the mule coin in the museum." Jake leaned forward. "He wants all of them. He's already got two. The one in the museum would be the last one he needs to complete the collection."

"So where does Miss Underwood come into this?"

"He forced her to help him by threatening to ruin her son—nephew—David Rush."

"What do you mean son?" Chief Baker threw up a hand.

"It's a long story." Jake shook his head. "Charles Amory has Rush and forced her to get the coin for him. She just got back from dropping it off somewhere. Please. I need to talk with her."

"I don't know about any of this. Why haven't you told me?"

"I haven't had a chance." Jake stood and leaned on the Chief's desk. "Please. Let me finish this, and when it's done, you can do whatever to me."

Chief Baker glared at him. "They're in interview room two. You better keep me in the loop."

"Yes, sir." Jake dashed out the door and down the hall.

"Bad time. Can't talk right now." The words hung in the air. Mac stared at her phone. After a second, she raised her gaze to the circle of faces around her. She opened her mouth to speak.

"I'm sure Detective Sanders will let us know what is going on as soon as he can," Miss P said.

So was she, but a sense of urgency filled her soul. Mr. Big traveled the streets of her town a free man while she drank coffee. "I can't sit here any longer. Sorry, Sam." Mac pushed to her feet. "Miss P, I want to go to the museum."

"I'm coming with you." Sam closed her computer and set it aside.

"Oh, no." Alan blocked his wife from getting out of the recliner. "This time, I'm exercising my veto as your caregiver, husband, and father of our baby. It's too soon."

"He's right." Mac placed a hand on her partner's shoulder. "I promise to keep you posted. Stay by your computer in case I need any information." Her stomach clenched as the vision of Sam crumpled on the bathroom floor flashed across her mind. She wrapped an arm around her abdomen.

"Okay." Understanding shone on Sam's sweet face. "I'll be here for back-up."

Mac flashed her a quick smile and left before she ended up in tears again. Miss P waited in the car for her and put it in gear as soon as she clicked her belt.

"Does Detective Sanders know where we're going?"

"I'm texting him now." She punched in a message and swiped a thumb up the screen.

"I'm not sure he will approve."

"Probably not, but I can't sit back and wait to see what

happens. I must warn Mrs. White." She gazed back at her partner's house. "Has Sam ever read your mind, Miss P?"

"She has a gift, but it's not mind reading, my dear. Sam has a remarkable talent for reading people—their body language, facial expressions, and tone of voice. She'd be a tremendous help to the police when they are conducting an interview, or a law firm would pay her well to help them with jury selection."

"But she knows what I'm thinking."

"She merely puts what she's observing with her knowledge of you and events and comes to a logical conclusion."

"You make it sound so clinical."

"I don't mean it to be." Miss P patted Mac's arm. "There's nothing clinical about Sam. She's a remarkable young lady."

"Yes, she is. She'll make a great mother." Sadness rippled through her. Change was coming, and while Mac looked forward to being "auntie" to a precious baby girl, she prayed her friend would still be at her side solving cases.

"Do not borrow trouble, my dear. Life has a way of working out for the best."

Mac barked a laugh. "Now look who's reading minds." Her phone rang. Zoe.

"I can't find David anywhere."

"Stop for now and meet us at the historical museum. It's urgent."

"I can be there in ten minutes."

"Do you have a plan in mind, Mackenzie?" Miss P asked.

"Not beyond warning Mrs. White. I'm hoping together we can think of something."

"Might I suggest a possible course of action?"

Mac turned to her. "I'm all ears."

CHAPTER 40

J ake stepped into the interview room. Walker raised an eyebrow at him but remained silent.

"Have you found David?" Katherine Underwood jumped to her feet.

He shook his head and pulled a chair even with the other man.

"Sit down, Ms. Underwood," Detective Walker said in a stern tone.

Katherine Underwood sat, her arms wrapped tightly about her waist. "I don't understand it. He said he'd release him." She murmured as she rocked in her chair.

"Who said he'd release him?" Walker asked.

"Charles Amory."

Gone was the confident, sassy woman Jake met on his first visit to the condo. "Where did you leave the mule coin?"

She raised eyes that had lost sight of hope to his. "Under a bench in the park by the river. He said to leave it and go. He said he'd release David a half hour later. But ..."

"Tell us about Amory."

"What do you want to know?"

"Where did he take you on your dates? Did he talk about any place he liked to go?"

She screwed her nose up like she'd smelled something disgusting. "We never went on dates. He met me different places to tell me what he wanted."

"Where?"

She passed a trembling hand across her brow. "I can't think right now."

"What about places he liked to go? We know he walked his dog in the park in the mornings."

"His dog?" She furrowed her brow at them. "I wasn't aware he had a dog."

Another lie. Jake clenched his teeth.

"Wait. I do remember him saying he was dog sitting for a neighbor." Katherine waved a hand in the air in a feeble gesture.

Adrenaline pumped through his veins. "Did he say which neighbor?" He shared a look with Walker.

"I wasn't paying attention."

"I'm going to step out for a moment. You think about where we might find Amory."

"I'll try." She slumped forward, her head in her hands.

In the hall, Jake extracted his phone from his pocket. "Get men down to the condos on the river. Have them go door to door. We're looking for Charles Amory. I'll text a photo. If someone answers other than Amory, ask if they know who's out of town but has a dog sitter."

"Yes, sir."

"Let me know as soon as you find anything." A long shot, but if they found Amory or the people on vacation, they might find David as well.

He had a text from Mac. His finger hovered over his text messages. Not now. Jake reentered the interview room and took his seat.

Katherine Underwood remained slumped in the same position as when he'd left. He looked at Walker, who shook his head. No change.

"Katherine." His tone demanded attention.

She raised her head.

"What part does Hank Young play in all of this?"

At the mention of Young's name, her face softened. "Poor Hank. I believe he really does care for me."

"Did you use him for information?"

"I had no choice. How else could I find out how the investigation was going and if the coin had been found?"

"Was he the one who told you I had it?" As he'd intended. The part he hadn't planned on was Vic getting shot.

"Yes." Tears followed the creases in her cheeks and neck. "Please. He didn't know anything. He trusted me."

"Who killed Freddy Koenig?"

"Charles Amory."

"Why did you let him frame your nephew?"

"I had no choice." She lifted her arms in a pleading gesture. "He promised me David would never be charged. He said you would realize he'd been framed before it got that far, and by that time, he—Charles—would be out of the country."

"And you believed him."

"Yes." She buried her face in her hands. "God help me, I did. What have I done?"

"Who has Amory been dog sitting for? Think, Katherine. It's important."

She straightened and ran a trembling hand across her brow. "It must be someone in his block of condos. I don't believe he's acquainted with anyone in the other block." She let out a frustrated sigh. "I don't have a clue."

"One last question. Does Amory know the historical museum has a mule coin?"

Katherine froze, her eyes wide with sudden understanding. After a moment, she nodded.

"Okay." Jake stood. "We'll stop now. Katherine Underwood, we're arresting you as an accessory in the theft of the time capsule memorabilia, attemped murder of a police officer, and the murder of Freddy Koenig." He nodded to the officer standing in back. "Inform Ms. Underwood of her rights and take her to a cell where she can lie down."

She grabbed his sleeve as he passed. "Please let me know if you hear anything about David."

The misery in her eyes broke through his stoney exterior, and compassion squeezed his heart. "I will."

Once behind his desk, he checked his text messages. He pushed to his feet. Mac was at the museum. His pulse pounded in his ears. Why hadn't he read this earlier?

"Good idea, Ms. P, but I don't have a silver dollar to replace the mule coin with." Mac pulled on her gloves and prepared to exit the car. "And I don't want to take the time to go to the bank."

"But I do." The elderly lady plucked one from her purse and slid it out.

"I should have guessed." Mac chuckled. "Now all we have to do is convince Mrs. White to go along with our scheme—your scheme."

They crunched across the hard packed snow to the museum entrance where Mrs. White waited to let them in.

"I've closed the museum like you asked until we had a chance to meet." She took their coats. "You sounded so urgent on the phone, Mackenzie."

"I'm afraid it is." She trailed after the historian to her office where she indicated Miss P. "This is—"

"I know Prudence." Mrs. White gave her a sweet smile. "How are you, my dear?"

"Quite well. I've been working with Mackenzie and Samantha for the past year as a research assistant and general girl Friday."

"How exciting."

"It is. We're here today about the mule coin." Miss P turned to Mac.

"We have reason to believe someone wants to possess all the coins. Including yours." Mac folded her hands in her lap. "You may be in danger."

Mrs. White raised a hand to her mouth. "I don't know what to say."

"We—Miss P—came up with a plan. If you'd like to hear it."

"Go on."

"What if we substituted a regular half dollar for the mule coin, and I put the real mule coin in my safe deposit box at the bank? Only temporarily of course."

"Won't the thief realize the switch?"

"Maybe, but we're counting on him being more worried about not getting caught." Mac leaned forward. "But we'd like you to take a vacation for a time. Stay away from here."

Mrs. White ran her eyes over the shelves and walls of her office. "I've got a lot of memories here. I'd hate to lose them to vandalism."

Mac thought about her own office and the things she held

dear. Some things others would see as trash, but they meant a lot to her. She straightened. "What if you told everyone your office was due to be repainted? You could box up your things and move them to a storage room for now. Take a week off and leave your office wide open for the thief to try his hand."

"That might work." She brightened. "I'll start right away." She rose and went to the safe. "Here's the mule coin. I'm trusting you, Mackenzie, to keep it safe until this business is all over."

Miss P handed her the regular half dollar and placed the mule coin in a baggie for Mac, who slipped it inside an inner pocket of her jacket. "Now, my dear, we must go to the bank."

Someone hammered on the door to the museum.

"Zoe. Mrs. White, would you let her in, but please don't tell her anything about switching the coins."

"Hi, Mac. Miss P. What's up?" Zoe's blonde curls framed a strained face. "Any news on David?"

Mac shook her head. Truth was, she'd forgotten about David's disappearance. "But I know Jake's got men out there looking for him." She prayed she wasn't telling the girl a lie.

"What's so urgent here?"

"We know who's behind all this. Charles Amory. He wants to own all the mule half dollars in existence. He's already got two, but there's a third here at the museum."

"Is he the one who framed David?" Zoe's eyes darkened.

"Yes." Mac touched her arm to get her attention. "But right now, I need you to help Mrs. White pack her office. She needs to get out of there fast. We think it won't be long before Amory comes for the last mule coin, which is in her safe."

"I hope he shows up while I'm here." The fury behind her words radiated off her body.

"He's dangerous, Zoe. Don't try anything on your own. Look at me." Mac projected her most demanding tone.

Zoe blinked.

"I mean it." Mac fixed her in a brown-eyed vise. "Promise me."

"I promise." She heaved a sigh. "Mrs. White, we'd better get started."

"Started doing what?" A male voice sounded behind them.

CHAPTER 41

Mac stood there as though fastened to the floor. It was as if the mere mention of his name had made Charles Amory appear. Now he directed a pistol at them from six feet away. How had he gotten in?

"I forgot to lock the door," Mrs. White said in a tremulous whisper.

"It's okay." Mac pushed the words past the lump of fear in her throat. "We know why Mr. Amory is here. Don't we?"

"Yes, Ms. Love. After I secure the rest of you, Mrs. White will get me the mule coin from her safe, and I will be on my way."

"You framed David." Zoe strode toward Amory.

The sound of a shot rang out. Bits of plasterboard showered down on them.

"Next time, I won't miss."

His emotionless voice made Mac's skin crawl.

"Stay calm, Zoe." She glared at Amory. "You don't have to tie us up. Mrs. White will get you what you want, and you can leave."

"Sure she will, and while she's at it, she'll alert the police too." His mouth lifted in a menacing, sarcastic smile. "We'll do things my way." He motioned for them to sit down and handed zip ties to Mrs. White. "Tie them up. Start with blondie. Hands behind their backs. One at their ankles too. Make sure they're tight."

As Mrs. White approached Zoe with the restraints, the agile blonde woman exploded from her chair and launched herself at Charles Amory. He fired once more.

Nerves at full stretch, Mac sensed what was about to happen before it did. She tackled Zoe as she flew past her and felt a searing pain in her right leg. They landed with a crash against the opposite wall, Mac on top. She bit her lip to keep from fainting.

"Look what you've done." Miss P knelt by her side. "Mac."

"She should have let me shoot the other one. Mrs. White, get me the coin."

Zoe squirmed beneath her. "Help me get free, Miss P."

"No. Stay where you are. You've done enough damage for one day." Miss P struggled to her feet and took a step closer to Amory, her hands in her capacious coat pockets as if searching for her phone. "I need to call an ambulance. Let me at least do that."

"When I'm gone, you can get all the help you need."

Mrs. White handed him a baggie with a shiny silver half dollar in it. He stuffed it in his pocket and scanned their faces.

"I've changed my mind." He raised the gun.

A loud bang echoed in the hall. Charles Amory stared first in amazement at the red stain spreading rapidly on the front of his shirt, and then at the revolver Miss P held in her hand.

"I suggest you drop your pistol unless you want me to fire on you again. With help, you have a chance of surviving, but if I am forced to shoot you again, you will certainly die."

The pistol thudded to the floor, and he staggered to a bench against the wall.

"Now I will call for help." She kicked the pistol behind her.

Zoe heaved Mac to the side, jumped to her feet, and in one swift move, scooped the pistol from the floor and aimed at Amory. Miss P grabbed her arm and jerked it upward as three shots rang out. Framed photographs shattered above his head, and the acrid smell of gunpowder filled the space. Mrs. White collapsed into a chair and wept into her hands.

Mac gritted her teeth against the pain in her leg and pushed herself to a sitting position against the wall. Charles Amory lay on the bench, his body covered with broken glass.

Miss P took the gun from Zoe's hand. "It's over, my dear."

GUNSHOTS. Inside the museum. Jake's heart pounded in his chest like a bass drum. Mac was in there. As he led his men through the door and down the hall, her chestnut eyes and soft lips filled his vision. *Please, God, don't let anything happen to her.*

He assessed the scene outside Mrs. White's office in a matter of seconds. Mac hurt but alert. Propped against the right wall. Amory down, laying on the bench to the left. Mrs. White out of the way.

But Miss P was the one who stopped him in his tracks. The woman stood straight ahead with two guns at her feet and her arms around Zoe. What went on here? He holstered his gun.

"Check on Amory." Jake gestured toward the prone man before crossing to Mac. "How bad is it?"

"Not bad, I think, but it really hurts." She grimaced.

Jake murmured a short prayer of gratitude. Something he had a feeling he'd be doing a lot if he and Mackenzie kept dating.

"I've called 911, Detective," Miss P said. "They should be arriving any minute."

"He's alive, sir."

"Good. See if you can get him to tell you where Rush is before the ambulance arrives."

Zoe pushed away from Miss P. "What did you say?"

He'd forgotten. None of them knew. "Charles Amory kidnapped David Rush."

"I almost killed him." Zoe fell into Miss P's arms once more. "I could have ruined the only chance of finding David."

"You shot him?" Jake stared at her.

"No, Detective Sanders, I did," Miss P said. "Zoe merely shot at him. She missed."

"He was going to kill us." Mac touched his arm. "Miss P saved us."

"I can't wake him up." The officer stood. "He's unconscious."

The wail of the approaching ambulances reached them.

"Bag the guns." Jake pushed to his feet. "What about the mule coin? Did Amory get it?"

"He thought he had, but we had substituted it for a standard silver half dollar before he arrived." Miss P released Zoe and smoothed her dress. "I believe the real coin is in Mackenzie's jacket pocket."

"Clever." Jake eyed her. "Your idea, no doubt?"

She didn't answer, but a rosy hue touched her wrinkled cheeks.

"These officers will get your statements." Mac passed by, strapped to a gurney. "I'll be at the hospital if you need me."

"Please tell her I will be there as soon as I can."

Jake pushed past the forensics team and hurried to his SUV. A carpet of gray clouds covered the sky, and the air smelled of snow. The two ambulances turned on their sirens and left the museum parking lot.

He'd been so worried about Mac he hadn't checked on Amory himself. What if he died? Jake had an idea where he might be holding Rush. But if he was ready to kill the four women without a thought, what chance was there of finding the kidnapped man alive? And if that were the case, he could be anywhere.

Jake put a call into the precinct and asked for the Chief. "We got a problem."

"Just once I'd like to hear something positive from you." The Chief's gravelly voice filled the air.

"I found Charles Amory."

"But?"

"He's been shot and is on his way to the hospital. Unconscious."

"Who shot him?"

"Miss P."

"My old chemistry teacher? This is not the time for jokes, Sanders."

"I'm not, sir." Jake pictured his chief's beet-red face. "I don't have the whole story, but it seems she saved the lives of at least four people."

"The woman was a powerhouse when I was young. It sounds like age hasn't changed her a bit. Is that it?"

"No. We still need to find David Rush."

"I may be able to help you. A report came in from the search a few minutes ago. Let me find it."

Jake pulled into a parking space at the hospital and watched as Mackenzie and Charles Amory were unloaded from the ambulances. "I need to get inside, sir."

"I'll find it and send it along, but you should have gotten it too. Keep me posted."

"Yes, sir."

Another patrol car pulled up, and two officers entered the emergency room. Jake pulled his coat around him and followed.

"I'll need you two to guard our suspect." Jake approached the desk and displayed his badge. "We're here to see the man and woman you just admitted. Charles Amory and Mackenzie Love."

She furrowed her brow at her computer screen. "Mr. Amory was taken to surgery, and Miss Love is in room eight."

"Where's surgery?"

"Second floor, but you can't—"

"The man's dangerous. We won't interfere with his surgery, but we need to be close by."

"Take the second set of elevators. Here's the code to operate them." She passed a piece of paper across the desk.

Jake memorized the numbers and handed it to his officers. "Get up there. I'll check on Mac and join you in a few minutes."

He pushed Mac's door open and stopped. Her beautiful eyes were closed, and a soft murmur escaped her lips as her chest rose and fell. He moved to the side of her bed and caressed her dark hair fanned out on the pillow. "I love you, Mackenzie Love," he whispered.

Her smile came warm and dreamy. "I love you too, Jake Sanders." She encircled his neck with a slim arm and pulled him down for a kiss. "I think we should get married."

"Married?" He tried to stand, but she had him firmly locked in her embrace. He'd never said anything about marriage.

She kissed him again. A long, lingering kiss that scrambled his brain.

Maybe marriage wasn't such a bad idea after all. At least that way he could keep tabs on her. "I think you're right. Mackenzie, will you marry me?"

"I thought you'd never ask."

The door opened. "Sorry."

"It's okay, doctor, he's my finance ... my fancy ..." Mac grinned.

"We're engaged." Jake stepped back and pulled on his earlobe.

"Congratulations." The doctor moved to the side of the bed. "I gave Miss Love a painkiller before sewing up her leg."

Jake shared an understanding look with him.

"There was damage to the muscle, and it will take time to heal. She'll need to stay off it for a few days. Afterward, she'll need to use crutches, and eventually, a cane until it fully mends." He removed some papers from his clipboard and handed them to Jake. "I'll need to see her in a week."

"Got it."

A light snoring sounded from the bed between them.

Jake's phone rang as the doctor slipped out the door. "Sanders."

"We've got a problem."

CHAPTER 42

J ake rushed from the room. "I'm on my way up."

"No need sir. Amory died in surgery. We're coming down."

Jake raked a hand through his hair. With Amory dead, how would they find David Rush? The email from the Chief. He swiped his screen open.

At first glance, the report of the condo search seemed to yield nothing, but he read it again. At one of the condos, the officers got no answer, but they heard a dog barking his head off inside. Jake noted the address.

"Back to the station house?" One of the officers asked.

"No. Do you have Amory's wallet and keys?"

"Yes, sir."

"Good. Follow me." Jake hurried to his SUV. He radioed for back-up on his way.

He didn't really need sirens and lights, but something about the situation seemed to demand it. Knowing Amory, anything was possible. Rush could bleed out before Jake got there.

The row of condos came into sight, and a police vehicle sat in front of one near the end. Jake screeched to a halt behind it. "Which of you is the dog guy?"

"I am, sir." One officer held up a bag of treats and a muzzle.

Jake held his hand out for Amory's keys. If his hunch was right, one of them should open the condo's front door. "Let's go." He knocked and called out "police" before inserting a key in the lock. After two tries, he found it.

The barking intensified at the sound of the knob turning. Jake gave the officer with the muzzle a nod and cracked the door.

"Good boy." The soothing voice of the officer seemed to have an effect. He held the bag of treats out for the short-haired terrier to smell. "Sit."

The barking stopped, and the dog obeyed. Jake opened the door a little wider.

The officer stepped into the gap and offered the brown and white dog a treat. The animal took it and trotted over to a rug nearby. The officer followed, speaking to the dog in a low voice. "I think he's fine now, sir." He hooked a leash to the terrier's collar and led him outside.

"Split up." Jake and the others hurried inside. "We could be looking for a body." He took the stairs two at a time. If Amory kept Rush here, it would probably be upstairs, and he prayed the man was still alive.

Five closed doors confronted him when he reached the top. He strode to the one on his left. An office. One closet. Packed with boxes. Nowhere to hide a body. Next, a linen closet. The third, a bathroom. Small closet. Fourth, a guest bedroom. A shape on the bed.

He flipped the light switch. Nothing. Dim light shown from a bedside lamp. A pile of clothes? Jake pulled the curtains off the window to allow the halfhearted winter sunlight into the room and turned to inspect the bed once more. The bundle of discarded clothes moved.

"David, it's Detective Sanders. Help is on the way." Relief washed over him. Jake ran to the door and called to his men. "I found him. Get an ambulance." He returned to the bed.

"Not—"

"Don't try to speak."

A hand grabbed his arm with amazing strength. Jake moved blankets away from a bloody face. Hank Young. A cold dread filled his body.

Two officers entered the room.

"Stay with him." Jake pushed past them. One room left.

He grabbed the doorknob and pushed. Locked. He drove his boot into the door, and it flew open. Another bed with another pile of clothes and blankets. Jake yanked his flashlight from his pocket and uttered a quick prayer as he approached the bed.

He shone the light on the pale face. David Rush. But he didn't respond. Jake pressed his fingers against the cool skin of his neck. The hint of a pulse against his fingertips. "You're safe, David. Help is on the way." Jake went to the door. "I've got Rush. He's alive."

"The ambulance should be here soon."

"Send them in here first." Jake returned to Rush's side and whispered in his ear. "Hang in there. Zoe's waiting for you."

For the second time that day, Jake followed two ambulances to the hospital. Not one of his best days.

"With you around, Detective Sanders, I don't have to worry about job security," the girl at the emergency desk said.

That did not make him feel better. He scrubbed a hand down his face.

"Press the button, please." He needed to see Mac.

"Miss Love isn't here. She was released a half hour ago."

"Who picked her up?"

"Some other young man."

Why didn't she call him? Or text? She'd give him you-know-what if the situation had been reversed. Jake stomped off.

"But she left you this." The nurse waved a piece of folded paper in her hand.

"Thanks." Jake snatched it from her and left. At his SUV, he read her message. Her phone was dead. Alan took her home where Miss P would stay with her. He took a deep breath and let his frustration drain. He punched one on his phone.

"Jake, I'm sorry I couldn't call."

Mac's voice sounded stronger and more like herself.

"No problem." Jake put a smile into his words. "How are you feeling?"

"It hurts, but I'll manage." She hesitated. "Jake, can I ask you something?"

"Sure."

"I got kind of loopy on the painkiller ..." She paused. "Did you ... say what I think you said?"

He chuckled. "You mean you don't remember?"

"Jake Sanders, now I know you did." Her voice rang with joy that warmed his heart. "I love you."

"I love you more." Everything else about his day faded away. At least for a moment. "I've got reports to write, but I'll be by later."

"I'll be waiting. Miss P will stay with me until my sisters can get here. I'm following the doc's orders and taking it easy for a few days."

"Good, but why are both sisters coming in?"

"We've got some business to settle." A serious tone sounded in her words. "And this is the perfect opportunity."

"Okay." But the detective in him couldn't help wondering what she wasn't telling him.

CHAPTER 43

Apprehension pricked her nerves. Now that she was engaged to Jake, he deserved to know about her past, but what if he couldn't accept it? Would he call it off before it became official? She leaned back on the pillows behind her head.

Three days of inactivity loomed ahead of her like three years. Afterward, crutches, but at least she'd be mobile. Hopefully. She'd never used crutches before, and she wasn't particularly athletic. She prayed for supernatural healing.

"Do you need anything, my dear?" Miss P fussed with her pillows and straightened her quilt.

"Maybe more tea?"

"Of course." She retrieved the cup from Mac's bedside table. "When do you expect your sisters to arrive? Not that I need to rush away, mind you. I am perfectly content to stay and care for you myself."

"I know you are." Mac gave her a warm smile meant to span the distance between them. "We've got an issue to take care of, and this is a good time. Kate and Beth should be getting here around seven this evening. They want to beat the storm coming in tomorrow morning."

"In about two hours." Miss P consulted her wristwatch. "I'll make us something to eat."

"Miss P ..." The desire to confide in her dear friend flooded through her.

"Yes?" The older woman turned with a soft smile.

"I have something to tell you about myself." Mac drew in a deep breath and let it out. "I only hope you still care about me after you hear what I'm about to say."

"If it has anything to do with who you really are, I already know. I've known since your parents moved here." She sat on the bed.

"You have?"

"Yes." She patted Mac's knee through the covers. "As a result of my past work for the government, I was asked to ... ease the transition for you and your parents into life in Washington."

"You knew all along?" Mac stared at her. "Why didn't you say something when my parents were killed?"

"I couldn't." Her eyes grew dark with sorrow. "I didn't want to risk putting you or your sisters' lives in jeopardy." She shrugged. "Time passed, and you all seemed to be doing well."

"We were." Mac lifted her gaze to the ceiling. "Until last year when Rosa Lombardi showed up."

"What's wrong, my dear?"

"It seems we're Rosa's cousins, and she's left her inheritance to us—the real us. The Rialto sisters. But if we come forward and accept it, we could be putting ourselves in the cross hairs of the mob." Mac lowered her gaze to her friend's wrinkled face. "What should we do?"

"I've spent so many years worried about your safety that I'm inclined to say let it go." Miss P removed her glasses and rubbed her nose. "But, I know the money is much needed for your business, and I'm sure your sisters could make good use of their portions as well. Give me some time to work on this puzzle."

"We don't have much time left. We have a deadline of one year from the time of Rosa's death to come forward. That's why we're meeting now." Mac touched Miss P's arm. "I'm glad I said something to you, and I'm glad you know."

"Secrets are terrible burdens to carry." The older woman gave her a gentle smile. "I'm glad we had this conversation as well. I would suggest you do the same with Detective Sanders. After all, he is your fiancé."

"How did you ...? Never mind." Mac gave a soft chuckle.

The doorbell chimed.

"If I'm not mistaken, there's the young man now." Miss P stood and smoothed the quilt on Mac's bed.

A sense of tingling delight flowed through her like she hadn't felt since the beginning of their relationship, and she couldn't wait to see him. When he appeared, she experienced a flash of heat from her toes to the top of her head. Their eyes locked as he crossed the room, and when he bent to kiss her, she met his lips half-way.

His mouth moved over hers with exquisite tenderness again and again. Until finally, with a sigh, he released her and pulled a chair close to the bed. "Hi."

"Hi to you too." She brushed a hand through his hair. "Bad day?"

"Yeah. My partner got shot. My fiancé was shot. My suspect died in surgery. Two other guys are pretty beat up. I think my boss is ready to fire me." He laid his head on the bed next to her.

"You're not serious about the Chief firing you, are you?"

"Probably not." He raised his head. "But I think the promotion to Detective Sergeant is off the table."

"None of it was your fault." She pushed herself up to a sitting position, but the pain in her leg made her slump back down.

"No." He inspected her face. "How are you?"

"Fine. It hurts a little, but not much."

"Uh-huh."

"Jake." She steeled herself to talk to him. "There's something you should know about me before we get officially engaged."

"Okay. I can't think of anything that would change my mind, but go ahead."

"I'm not Mackenzie Love. My real name is Elizabeth Rialto. My family came here under witness protection."

"As in the Rialto sisters who inherited from Rosa Lombardi?"

"Yes." Mac couldn't read his face. Was he upset? Shocked? Mad? "I didn't know until last Thanksgiving when Beth told me. The inheritance is why they're coming now. We have to decide about whether to come forward and accept it."

He rose and paced the room, stopping in front of a photo of the two of them taken about a month ago. He carried it back to the bed. "Are you this woman?" He pointed to her image.

"Yes, of course." What was he getting at?

"Then you're Mackenzie Love. You may have been born Elizabeth Rialto, but now you're Mackenzie Love." He placed a hand on her cheek. "You're the woman I fell in love with. The woman I want to marry."

"Yes." And for the first time in months, Mac felt at peace. "I'm Mackenzie Love."

"I'm sorry to interrupt." Miss P cracked the door open a few inches. "Beth has been trying to reach you without success."

"I turned my phone off." Mac retrieved her cellphone from the bed. "I'll call her."

"No need, dear. We talked, and she asked me to tell you they will not be arriving tonight. There is a snowstorm coming through Kansas City, and they will wait until the roads have been cleared in the morning."

She swallowed the sudden lump of disappointment that rose in her throat.

"I assured her I would stay with you for as long as you needed me, and not to worry." Miss P gave her a soft smile. "I have dinner ready."

"Thanks. Give me a minute." Mac reached for Jake's hand and raised her eyes to his. She hadn't realized how much she'd been looking forward to seeing her sisters that evening. As she gazed at the wonderful man sitting next to her, worry rode the wave of disappointment into her heart, and she wondered anew if her confession would change the way he felt. "Are you sure we're okay?"

"We're perfect." He kissed her once more with renewed passion.

Afterwards, she stroked his face. "Stay for dinner."

"Not tonight." He stood. "You need to rest."

"Wait. You didn't tell me if you found David Rush."

"We did." His smile dissolved. "And Hank Young. They were both in bad shape."

"How could one man be so evil?" Her chest ached as if it would split open. "Charles Amory destroyed so many lives."

"All he cared about was money."

"The mule coin from the museum." She struggled to sit up. "It's in my jacket pocket."

"I have it. Along with the other two. Get some rest." His soothing voice smoothed the wrinkles in her soul. "You and your sisters have a big decision to make. We'll talk more tomorrow."

"What do you think we should do?"

He studied her a moment and walked over to her armchair in the corner of the room. When he returned, he laid her Bible on the table next to her. "Do what you always do. Find the answer in here." He kissed the top of her head. "I love you."

"I love you too."

Mac picked up her Bible. It fell open to the book of Jeremiah, chapter forty-two. She began to read, and when she got to verses eleven and twelve, she couldn't believe her eyes. There was her answer.

"'Do not fear the king of Babylon anymore,' says the Lord. 'For I am with you and will save you and rescue you from his power. I will be merciful to you by making him kind, so he will let you stay here in your land.'"

Somehow, she and her sisters would be able to claim the inheritance from their cousin, Rosa Lombardi, without fear. She returned her Bible to the table beside her bed and closed her eyes.

CHAPTER 44

The aroma of fresh brewed coffee drew her out of her dreams and into the light of day. Mac kept her eyes closed and savored the state between fully awake and the edge of sleep when her body felt completely relaxed and perfectly content.

The smells of bacon and toast wafted into her bedroom, and her stomach growled. A clamor of voices sounded in the hallway, and she was fully awake. Her sisters had arrived.

"We drive over three hours in treacherous conditions to see our poor, injured sister and she's sleeping like a baby." Kate stood at the foot of Mac's bed with her hands on her hips. "Were you really shot, or did you make it up to get us to come to you?"

"I've got the stitches to prove it." Mac chuckled. "Want to see?"

"No way." Her middle sister put her hands in front of her face. "You know how squeamish I am about stuff."

"How did you ever take care of your kids when they were little?"

"I didn't. I sent them next door to my friend, the nurse."

"Where's Beth?"

"She's unpacking. I live out of my suitcase, so I don't have to."

Mac shook her head and grinned. A woman with short gray hair came in and bent to give her a hug.

"Are you in pain?"

"She was sleeping when I came in," Kate said.

"She's probably exhausted." Beth threw her middle sister a scowl and stroked Mac's hair.

"I'm fine, Beth." Mac took her oldest sister's hand. "It only hurts when I move. But, in a couple of days, I'll be up hobbling around again."

"Breakfast is served, ladies." Miss P appeared in the doorway. "I'll bring yours in momentarily."

"We'll eat in here with Mac. Have you got any tray tables?"

"Yes. Let me show you."

After all the women were finished eating, Miss P collected the plates. "I think it's time you decide what to do about your inheritance, ladies. I'll be in the kitchen."

"She knows?" Beth stared at Mac.

"I told her last night. She's a close friend, and she's wise." Mac sighed. "I told Jake too."

"What?" Kate threw up her arms. "I thought we agreed not to tell anyone."

"Jake asked me to marry him. I couldn't say yes without telling him the truth." She glared at her sisters. "Your husbands know, don't they?"

"Okay. I get it." Kate grinned. "Congratulations, by the way."

"Thanks." A matching grin split Mac's face, and a bubble of joy rose inside her.

"Congratulations, baby sister." Beth moved her chair next

to the bed where she could reach out and touch her arm. "What advice did Miss P give you?"

"She said she'd have to think about it." Mac shrugged. "But Jake said I should look for the answer in the Bible, and he was right. It's behind you on the desk."

Beth handed it to Mac.

"Let me read what I found." She read to them from Jeremiah, chapter forty-two, verses eleven and twelve. "Doesn't it seem like it's saying we don't have to worry about the mob? That God will protect us?"

"It does." Kate leaned forward. "That's amazing."

"I don't know." Beth crossed her arms over her chest.

"Beth, come on."

"Come on?" She jumped to her feet. "You weren't the one who saw the mangled car with our parents' bodies. Or Daddy with the bullet hole in his head." She collapsed into her chair. "I couldn't go through that again if something happened to one of you. I'd ..."

Kate rushed to her side, and Mac reached for her hand.

"It's all right. Hush now." Kate looked at Mac over their sister's head.

With two boys in college, her middle sister could use the money as much as Mac could. But they agreed the decision had to be unanimous.

"Have we found out whether we can accept the inheritance anonymously?"

"Not yet. I'm waiting for a lawyer friend to get back to me," Kate said.

"I guess unless that's an option, we—" Mac's phone rang. She glanced at the screen. Who would be calling her from prison? She held up a hand to silence her sisters. "Mackenzie Love."

"This is the United States Penitentiary, Marion, Illinois. Will you accept a call from Luigi Bono?"

Her hand tightened around her cellphone as the image of a man with silver hair and a dark pinstripe suit flashed across her mind. Why would she want to speak with the man who caused her so much pain and still haunted her nightmares? And yet, she heard herself saying, "Yes." She punched speaker and motioned for her sisters to stay quiet.

"Miss Love?"

"What do you want?" She put as much steel into her trembling voice as she could.

"Ah. I see you remember me."

"How could I forget?"

"I haven't much time, so I'll get right to the point. I know you and your sisters are the heirs to Rosa Lombardi's fortune."

"How do you—?"

"I know many things, Miss Love. I also know you are concerned about accepting the inheritance, and why. I want to put your mind at ease. My ... friends are not interested in you or your sisters. In fact, your family has never been in danger from them. You are free to accept Miss Lombardi's money without fear."

"But my parents."

"My friends had nothing to do with the unfortunate death of your parents, Miss Love. My time is up."

"Wait. Why are you telling me this?"

"Let's just say I'm a new man. The old man has passed away. Good-bye."

Mac pressed End and stared at the phone.

"Do you believe him?" Kate asked.

She searched her heart for the answer. "Yes. I do."

"I've lived with this fear so long." Beth buried her head in her hands. "I'm not sure I know how not to."

"You'll learn, and the first step will be to accept our inheritance." Kate bounced around the room. "Praise the Lord."

"Yes." Beth straightened and looked at Mac. "What's the matter? I thought you'd be happy."

"I am." Mac flashed her a smile. It was an answer to prayer. No more money worries for the agency. But a nagging question threatened to ruin her joy. If the mob didn't kill their parents, who did?

The End

ACKNOWLEDGMENTS

It's always hard to know where to begin with honoring people who help me while I write a book. The truth is each one is equally important to me from the ones who take time to help make sure I get my facts straight to the ones who read the first draft and show me where I left out a word. It truly takes a village! I feel like every book should have the author's name on the cover followed by et al!

However, I do want to acknowledge by name some of the people who have helped me with this book. I begin with Detective Lieutenant Steve Sitzes of the Washington Police Department, Washington, Missouri. He took time to share his expertise with me and help me keep things as true to life as possible. If you find any mistakes, I take complete responsibility!

To my friend and mentor, DiAnn Mills, thank you for all your encouragement and support. I'm so thankful God brought us together.

And for Patricia Bradley, another good friend and encourager. Thank you.

To my Word Weaver posse, Bonnie Sue Beardsley, Starr Ayers, Denise Holmberg, Linda Dindzans, Caroline Powers, Charlsie Estes, plus Sandra Melville Hart. You are amazing! Your encouragement and support keeps me striving to be a better writer and a better person.

To Linda Fulkerson and all the Scrivenings Press family, I

feel blessed to be a part of such an excellent group of writers and encouragers. Thank you for all the prayers and support.

I would be remiss if I didn't mention my loyal readers! Thank you for continuing to read and share my books with your friends and family. You are amazing!

And of course, my sweet husband, Les. The love of my life and biggest fan. I thank God every day for him.

If I have forgotten someone, my humblest apologies. I assure you, your input was much appreciated. Unfortunately, the memory's not what it used to be!

About the Author

When Deborah Sprinkle retired, she had a plan for keeping busy. Part of that plan was to write a mystery novel.

After collaborating with Kendra Armstrong on her non-fiction book entitled *Exploring the Faith of America's Presidents*, Deborah turned her hand to fiction.

It took several years of honing her craft before Deborah realized her dream. *Deadly Guardian* debuted in May 2019, with Mantle Rock Publishers. Deborah's second book in the series, *Death of an Imposter*, came out November 24, 2020, and the third, *Silence Can Be Deadly*, November 2, 2021, both with Scrivenings Press.

Her new series debuted in 2022, with *The Case of the*

Innocent Husband. She also had a novella published that year and a short story in an anthology. Deborah continued to win awards for her short stories, articles, and flash fiction.

Deborah lives in Memphis with her greatest fan, her husband of 50+ years, and describes herself as an ordinary woman serving an extraordinary God.

MORE MAC & SAM MYSTERIES

The Case of the Innocent Husband

A Mac & Sam Mystery—Book One

Private Investigator Mackenzie Love needs to do one thing. Find out who shot Eleanor Davis. Or she'll have to leave town.

When Eleanor Davis is found shot in her garage, the only suspect, her estranged husband, is found not guilty in a court of law. However, most of the good citizens of Washington, Missouri, remain unconvinced. It doesn't matter that twelve men and women of the jury found him not guilty. What do they know?

And since Private Investigator Mackenzie Love accepted the job for the defense and helped acquit Connor Davis, her friends and neighbors have placed her squarely in the enemy camp. Therefore, her overwhelming goal becomes to find out who killed Eleanor Davis.

Or leave the town she grew up in.

As the investigation progresses, the threats escalate. Someone wants to stop Mackenzie and her partner, Samantha Majors, and is willing to do whatever it takes—including murder.

Can Mac and Sam find the killer before they each end up on the wrong side of a bullet?

Get your copy here:

https://scrivenings.link/innocenthusband

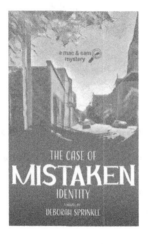

The Case of Mistaken Identity

A Mac & Sam Mystery—Book Two

Private Investigator Mackenzie Love manages to get into trouble on a simple shopping trip where she finds herself at the business end of a gun. It's clear her attacker mistakes her for someone else, but who? And why is her look-alike in so much trouble?

Mac enlists the help of her partners, Samantha Majors and Miss P, and Detective Jake Sanders to find her doppelgänger and solve the case of mistaken identity.

In the meantime, Mr. Fischer of Fischer Industries comes to the private detectives for help with a problem of his own. As Mac and Sam work on his case, they begin to wonder if the two cases are related.

Can Mac and Sam unravel the clues and get justice for both Mac's look-alike and Mr. Fischer?

Get your copy here:

https://scrivenings.link/mistakenidentity

TROUBLE IN PLEASANT VALLEY
SERIES BY DEBORAH SPRINKLE

Silence Can Be Deadly

Trouble in Pleasant Valley

Book Three

It started with a taxi ride ... or did it?

Forced from the career he loved and into driving a taxi, Peter Grace had grown accustomed to his simple life. Until one night when a suspicious fare and a traffic jam blew it all apart, and he was on the run again. Only this time it wasn't a matter of changing occupations but of life and death.

He needed help and he knew where to find it. His old friend Rafe in Pleasant Valley. What he didn't count on was finding not only the help he needed but a community of new friends and the love of his life. Zoe Poole.

The story of Captain Nate Zuberi and his wife Madison continues as they too risk their lives to help Peter. Along with Peter, Rafe, and Zoe, they strive to catch an assassin.

But can the group of friends find the killer before anyone else gets hurt?

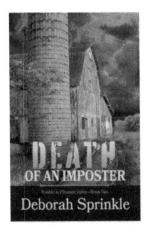

Death of an Imposter

Trouble in Pleasant Valley

Book Two

Her first week on the job and rookie detective Bernadette Santos has been given the murder of a prominent citizen to solve. But when her victim turns out to be an imposter, her straight forward case takes a nasty turn. One that involves the attractive Dr. Daniel O'Leary, a visitor to Pleasant Valley and a man harboring secrets.

When Dr. O'Leary becomes a target of violence himself, Detective Santos has two mysteries to unravel. Are they related? And how far can she trust the good doctor? Her heart tugs her one way while her mind pulls her another. She must discover the solutions before it's too late!

Deadly Guardian

Trouble in Pleasant Valley

Book One

Madison Long, a high school chemistry teacher, looks forward to a relaxing summer break. Instead, she suffers through a nightmare of threats, terror, and death. When she finds a man murdered she once dated, Detective Nate Zuberi is assigned to the case, and in the midst of chaos, attraction blossoms into love.

Together, she and Nate search for her deadly guardian before he decides the only way to truly save her from what he considers a hurtful relationship is to kill her—and her policeman boyfriend as well.

MORE FROM DEBORAH SPRINKLE

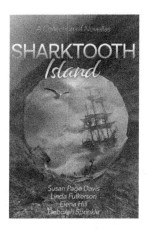

Sharktooth Island

A collection of Romantic Suspense novellas

A fabled island that no one dares to tame.

This collection contains four novellas:

Book 1 - Out of the Storm (1830) by Susan Page Davis

Laura Bryant sails with her father and his three-man crew on his small coastal trading schooner. After a short stay in Jamaica, where she meets Alex Dryden, an officer on another ship, the Bryants set out for their home in New England.

In a storm, they are blown off course east of Savannah, Georgia, to a foreboding island. Captain Bryant tells his daughter he's heard tales of that isle. It's impossible to land on, though it looks green and inviting from a distance. It has no harbor but is surrounded by dangerous rocks and cliffs.

Pirates outrun the storm and decide to bury a cache of treasure on this island and return for it later. On board is Alex, whom the cutthroats captured in Jamaica and forced to work for them. Alex risks his own life to escape the pirates and tries to help Laura and Captain Bryant outwit them. Beneath the deadly struggle, romance blossoms for Laura.

Book 2 - *A Passage of Chance (1893)* by Linda Fulkerson

Orphaned at a young age, Melody Lampert longs to escape the loveless home of the grandmother who begrudgingly raised her. Stripped of her inheritance due to her grandmother's resentments, Melody discovers her name remains on the deed of one property—an obscure island off the Georgia coast that she shares with her cousin. But when he learns the island may contain a hidden pirate treasure, he's determined to cheat her out of her share.

Ship's mechanic Padric Murphy made a vow to his dying father—break the curse that has plagued their family for generations. To do so, he must return what was taken from Sharktooth Island decades earlier—a pair of rare gold pieces. His opportunity to right the wrong arrives when his new employer sets sail to explore the island.

After a series of unexplainable mishaps occur, endangering Padric and his boss's beautiful cousin Melody, he fears his chance of breaking the curse may be ruined. But is the island's greed thwarting his plans? Or the greed of someone else?

Book 3 - *Island Mayhem (1937)* by Elena Hill

Louise Krause stopped piloting to pursue nursing, but when money got too tight she was forced to give up her dreams and start ferrying around a playboy who managed to excel during the Great Depression. When a routine aerial tour turns south, Louise is unable to save the plane.

After crash landing, the cocky pilot is stranded. She longs to escape the uninhabited island, but her makeshift raft sinks, and she and her companions are in even worse trouble. Can Louise learn to trust the others in order to survive, or will the island's curse and potential sabotage lead to her demise?

Book 4 - *After the Storm (present day)* by Deborah Sprinkle

Mercedes Baxter inherited two passions from her father—a love for

Sharktooth Island, a spit of land in the middle of the ocean left to her in his will, and a dedication to the study of the flora and fauna on and around its rocky landscape.

For the last five years, since graduating from college, Mercy led a peaceful, simple life on the island with only her cat, Hawkeye, for company. Through grant money she obtained from a conservancy in Savannah, she could live on her island while studying and writing about the plants and animals there. Life was perfect.

But when a hurricane hits the island, Mercy's life changes for good. Her high school sweetheart, Liam Stewart, shows up to help her with repairs, and ignites the flame that has never quite died away. And if that's not enough, while assessing the damage to the island, they make a discovery that puts both their lives in danger.

Scrivenings
PRESS
Quench your thirst for story.
www.ScriveningsPress.com

Stay up-to-date on your favorite books and authors with our free e-newsletters.

ScriveningsPress.com

Made in the USA
Middletown, DE
03 September 2024

60235290R00172